MW01134295

BATTLE OF THE ULTRAS

THE LAST HERO, BOOK 3

MATT BLAKE

MATTBLAKEAUTHOR.COM

If you want to be notified when Matt Blake's next novel is released, please sign up to his mailing list.

http://mattblakeauthor.com/newsletter

Your email address will never be shared and you can unsubscribe at any time.

[1]

Orion looked down at Saint and watched as a huge ball of energy spread out of his hands.

It was snowy. The streets of New York were empty. All around, Orion could hear screams. The screams of parents separated from their children. The screams of children finding their homes destroyed. So many screams.

He felt ashamed. Totally ashamed of his entire kind for allowing this to happen.

So ashamed of himself for not stopping Saint's trail of destruction sooner.

The air was thick with the smell of smoke. Orion's hands shook. He tasted blood on his lips. The battle with Saint had been long and arduous, a test of sheer endurance.

But it was ending right here. It was ending today.

One way or another, it would be all over soon.

It just didn't help that Saint floated right in front of Orion's son's house right now.

"You know what you have to do," Saint said. He was in his silver metal armor, dressed like a knight. All around him, a black cloud that followed him everywhere. A black cloud that terrified citizens, that you could identify from a mile away.

"We don't have to end things this way," Orion said.

Orion couldn't see Saint's face, as thicker blobs of snow fell down. But he knew Saint would be smiling. "I think you know this is exactly how we end it."

Orion looked around at the city. He saw smoke rising from distant buildings. Further away, he heard sirens and the rotors of approaching helicopters. He knew what the government would do to Heroes like him—or ULTRAs as they now called his kind. Sure, he'd helped them in their fight against Saint. But now they had a chance to get rid of them both in one swoop, Orion was certain they weren't going to hesitate.

"Lower your powers," Orion said. "Please."

Saint laughed. His cackle was deep enough to make even the strongest Hero's skin crawl. "Is that what it's come to, oh mighty powerful one? You begging me to lower my powers?"

"This has gone far enough—"

"No," Saint barked. His voice changed from amused to serious in an instant. "No it hasn't. And you know exactly where this is going if you don't do something about it. Fast."

Orion's skin crawled when he saw what Saint was looking at.

On the street below, there was a girl. A little girl running toward a little boy.

"Oh look," Saint said, gesturing toward Orion's right. "Our friends from the army are joining us. What a beautiful place for them to take us down."

"Don't bring those kids into this," Orion said.

"Then do what you have to do."

"Saint, I—"

"Do what you have to do!"

Orion watched the children run closer to one another. He saw the little grin on Kyle's face as he got closer to his sister. He felt a lump in his throat. He couldn't risk any kind of battle over this place. He had to risk flying into Saint. He had to fly into that shield of energy and teleport the pair of them far away from here, even if it killed him.

"Do it!" Saint shouted.

Kyle and Cassie got closer to one another.

"It's over, Saint."

"Maybe it is. Come on then. End it. End it all.

Orion didn't need telling again.

He flew at Saint faster than he'd ever flown at anyone in his entire life.

"Good-bye, old sport," Saint said.

As he got closer to Saint, within inches from his face, he swore he saw the smile appear from under his mask, as if it had turned translucent.

"Big mistake," Saint said.

He felt the ball of energy then. It crashed through his body, rippled all around him. He lost sense of all sights, all sounds. He lost sense of where he was, even, or where he was supposed to be taking Saint to.

And then he saw it.

He saw the scene beneath him.

He saw the buildings and homes that'd stood just moments ago, flattened.

He saw flames. Smoke.

But most of all, he saw Kyle Peters crouching over a body.

His sister's body.

He felt a pain in his chest. His legs went wobbly. He

wanted to go down there. He wanted to help Kyle. He wanted to help Cassie.

Then he felt a pain smack into his kidneys and he disappeared from Staten Island.

He appeared somewhere in the Sierra Nevada. Somewhere much warmer.

Saint was opposite him. His helmet had cracked a little around the jaw. He was smiling.

He stretched out his arms. "You did what you had to do. Killed a million New Yorkers in the process. But it saved your son so everything's okay. Right?'

Orion felt anger and fury build up within.

He flew at Saint and cracked a power-packed punch across his jaw. It was a punch strong enough to take the pair of them to the middle of the Pacific Ocean, hovering over it in a torrential rain storm.

Saint hit back and knocked Orion into the snow of Antarctica. He wrapped his hands tightly around Orion's neck and squeezed.

"You always cared about the boy more than the girl, though, didn't you? He was always the one you wanted to follow in your footsteps."

Orion screamed with pure anger as the sight of his fallen daughter filled his mind.

He flipped out of Saint's grip. Appeared above him. Fired balls of ice into him.

Saint just shook them off, rubbed his hands together and went crashing up into Orion.

But this time, Orion felt a ball of energy emit from his own body, much like the one that had fired out of Saint's back in Staten Island. It was tiring and waning, but it was still staggeringly powerful. It took everything out of him.

It knocked Saint down into the snow.

Saint lay there, writhing. His mask was off now. His totally burned face and head were on show.

He looked up at Orion with his green eyes. One of his arms had broken out of place. And as much as he tried to fix it, the arm just wasn't adjusting.

Orion used the little of his energy left to float down above Saint. To press his hand against his neck and push him back into the icy cold snow.

"My daughter," he said. "You... you killed my daughter."

"But she wasn't really *your* daughter, was she? Just like Kyle's not really your son. Not anymore."

"Don't you dare—"

"You gave them up. Gave them up because you were scared of the world they might have to live in if they knew what they were. Scared of what they might become when they discovered their true powers. What they are really capable of."

Orion saw the goading smile on Saint's face and he wanted to kill him. He knew Saint was weak. He could just *feel* his weakness in the air. But he wanted to make him weaker. "Stop."

"I won't stop. Not until I've destroyed you. Not until I've completely taken over this planet. And not until the day I've got Kyle Peters by *my* side, convinced that his own biological daddy was the one who destroyed the—"

"Stop this!" Orion tightened his grip around Saint's throat, not just with his hands but with his telekinesis, too.

But with the last of his strength, Saint resisted, as more and more snow covered him. He kept on smiling, blood rolling down his chin. "And his brother, too. The one you care about even less. The one you totally abandoned. The one that went wrong. I think he'll be a very crucial asset in the fight against you, whether you're still here or not."

Orion thought about the person Saint referred to. He felt guilt. Severe guilt. He hadn't intended to abandon any of his children. Something just went wrong with the third one. Something that made him... different. Different to the others. He could just feel it whenever he was in his presence.

"But for now, you live. Live with the knowledge of what you've done. Of the people you've killed."

"I haven't killed anyone."

Saint's smile widened. "You keep telling yourself that. You keep—"

Orion didn't listen to any more of what Saint said.

He squeezed his eyes shut.

Created a wormhole with every ounce of strength he had left.

"You won't come back from this," he said.

He looked into the dark mass ahead of him—the endless wormhole that he'd forged with so much strength that it would just go on and on in an eternal loop.

"You'll regret not killing me," Saint said, smiling.

Orion didn't reply. He didn't know what to say. Not anymore.

"I'm sorry you couldn't find your way," he said.

And then he threw Saint into the wormhole, into his eternal abyss.

When he closed the wormhole at this side, he fell back. Tasted blood on his lips.

He leaned back on the freezing ice and stared up at the perfect Antarctica sky. The snow fell down and covered his body. The wind howled, cold enough to freeze him within a few hours.

He didn't warm himself up.

He didn't teleport himself away.

All he could think about was the people he'd lost.

The casualties of battle.

And his daughter, lying there on the road in Kyle's arms.

He felt a tear roll down his cheek and freeze instantly as the last of his strength slipped away.

I hovered above the fallen city of Manchester, United Kingdom, and wondered how many more battles I'd have to fight, and whether there was even any point in fighting anymore.

The late afternoon clouds were thick. I'd heard a stereotype about the United Kingdom always being rainy and gloomy, and stories that Manchester was a particularly miserable place, weather-wise. Which was true, don't get me wrong. The city below was covered in darkness.

But a major part of that was the thousands of ULTRAbots hovering over it.

I was silent, and so too was everyone else. I looked back at the Resistance. Looked at Orion—who'd scrapped calling himself Bowler since everyone knew who he was now. I looked at the rest of the Resistance—Stone, Ember, Roadrunner, Vortex. The Resistance, or what was left of it after Slice and Aqua fell.

Then, I looked behind them. Looked at the other ULTRAs, hundreds of them, all of them hovering behind me and waiting for me to make the move. They were Nycto's ULTRAs. At least, the ones who'd decided to back the Resistance and me. Sure, some of them had defected to Saint's cause the second he floated back into the world. But we had enough. Enough to strike back.

At least I hoped.

"So can we go through the plan just one more time?" Stone asked. There was an excitement in his voice. An anticipation.

I bit down on my lip. I didn't have my mask anymore. Didn't need it now the entire planet knew who I was.

I looked down at the swarm of ULTRAbots. They were strong. Really damned strong.

But nothing we hadn't dealt with before.

"We smash some ULTRAbots and loosen their grip on this city," I said.

Stone grinned. He was well built, with a short buzz cut and bigger muscles than I'd ever seen. He cracked his solid rock fists together, the stone spreading up his arms as he did. "That's the kinda plan I'm into."

I looked at Vortex. She had long, ginger hair and a freckly face. She was skinny, and to see her on the street or at school, you'd be forgiven for thinking she was just your everyday outcast.

But Vortex wasn't an everyday outcast at all. She was an outcast, sure, but the complete opposite to an everyday one.

"You ready?" I asked.

She smiled, revealing her yellowy teeth. "Always ready to rain chaos."

Her head shot back. Her eyes rolled into her skull.

She shot a beam of energy down toward the ULTRAbots below.

"Let's go!"

The rest of the ULTRAs followed Vortex's beam toward the ULTRAbots. I knew when the beam had hit because I saw some of the ULTRAbots flinch. Some of them smacked the sides of their heads like they had something in their minds—whatever minds these machines had—that they just couldn't get rid of.

Which was exactly what happened when Vortex did her thing. She could create nightmares. Quite a handy trait.

"Remember our code," Orion called, as I pulled back my hands and readied myself to slam into the first of the ULTRAbots.

"Always," I said.

I knew what Orion's code was. What the Resistance's code was.

We don't kill our own.

I wasn't sure I'd be able to stick to that if I saw Saint. But I'd have to try.

The first ULTRAbots didn't even see me. I slammed into the middle of them, then sent a blast of ice flying into all their faces, knocking them out of the sky.

I grabbed the arm of the next ULTRAbot. Flew it into its friend as the other ULTRAbot lifted its gun.

Then I created a mini-wormhole in front of the ULTRAbot getting ready to fire.

Closed the wormhole right over by Ember, who was already under the attack of several ULTRAbots.

He looked down at me as the ULTRAbots around him exploded thanks to my wormhole. "I had them," he shouted, his hands covered in flames.

I tilted my head to one side as more ULTRAbots approached. The streets below were empty. I hoped it wasn't already too late to save Manchester. "I'd rather not take your word for it."

The three ULTRAbots at the front of the approaching crowd fired several heavy rounds at me. I dodged them, using everything I'd ever been angry about in my life to fuel my powers. I saw my sister Cassie dying in the Great Blast. I saw Nycto attacking the party venue last summer, Mike Beacon falling.

I saw Mom.

My powers got stronger whenever I thought of Mom. The gunshots of the surrounding ULTRAbots became irrelevant. Nothing seemed to matter, nothing at all.

Mom had been so kind. She'd been so strong. She'd been the rock of my family for so long, after Cassie's death sent my dad down a dark path.

And now she was gone. Killed, it turned out, on Saint's orders. A way of trying to break me down. Bring me to the edge.

Only I wasn't broken down. I was fighting back. And I wasn't going to stop until I killed Saint.

A crowd of ULTRAbots thickened around me. I couldn't see in any direction for their mass. Some of them were firing already, so I slowed the bullets in the air and shot them right back at them, or diverted them so they hit the rest of the surrounding ULTRAbots.

But as the bullets came closer to me, I knew I was going to have to try something different.

I let the bullets get nearer.

Let them get inches from my body.

And then I stopped them, just like that.

We looked at one another, me and the ULTRAbots. Looked at each other, suspended in reality.

"Bullets?" I said. "Seriously?"

Then I shot all the bullets back out at the ULTRAbots and took each and every one of them surrounding me down.

I saw a gap then. Saw some people on the street. Military, fighting back with guns. We could help them. We could get the citizens of Manchester out of this place, to somewhere safe, if need be. But preferably, we'd defend Manchester. We'd keep it standing.

I was about to teleport down to them when I saw a dark cloud in the distance.

It was a distinctive dark cloud. A cloud I'd seen before. One that could only belong to one ULTRA.

Saint.

"Kyle, wait!" Orion called.

I heard him, but I didn't *really* hear him. Not really.

Because as I looked at the dark cloud of Saint, I didn't just see an ULTRA. I saw the man who'd torn my family apart. The man who'd not only killed my mother, but killed my sister all those years ago too.

I felt the anger peaking inside me and I felt the need for revenge.

"Kyle!"

I looked back at the ULTRAs fighting off the ULTRAbots. Saw them all flying at one another, firing at one another. I wanted to stay. I wanted to help them.

And then I looked back at Saint as he got further away.

I couldn't let him go.

I had to make him pay.

"Kyle!" Orion shouted.

I heard him, but I didn't listen.

I took a deep breath and felt the anger of all my loss fill my body.

Then I fired myself in Saint's direction, leaving the Resistance behind to fight off the ULTRAbots, to fight for Manchester.

I had a personal mission to attend to.

[3]

I didn't even have to think whether or not to chase after Saint.

When you wanted to avenge the deaths of the people you loved so badly, you just did it, whether it seemed like a good idea or not. The time for sitting back and moping went away. It had to, or it'd tear you apart.

I wasn't letting it tear me apart. I wasn't letting Saint tear *anyone's* lives apart. Not anymore.

I flew in the direction of the dark cloud. The rain fell down heavier over Manchester now. Beside me, I saw smoking buildings. I saw cars in streets, smashed and abandoned. I'd seen so many scenes like this since Saint launched his attack on the world just three weeks ago. I'd seen so many big cities fall. Places you didn't think it was possible to fall. Paris. Rome. Washington. Beijing. Places of strength. Places of power.

All of them powerful no more. Not now they had a new leader. One ruling leader to unite them all in misery.

As I flew after Saint, I heard the Resistance and the ULTRAbots still fighting on above me, behind me. I felt guilty for leaving them, sure. But I had my own fight here. I had my own personal battle. And they were strong. They thought they needed me, but in truth, they could handle themselves.

And if I took down Saint, maybe they wouldn't have to handle themselves at all.

I pushed on even further, my body flying and teleporting through the air so fast that I could feel my stomach twisting. Every time I teleported to where I swore Saint was, I saw his dark cloud get further away. I felt him slipping from my grip...

But no.

That wasn't happening.

He wasn't getting away.

I smelled the smoke in the air as the breeze brushed against my bare face. Nycto had destroyed my Glacies mask before he was tossed aside like a fly by Saint. It didn't matter really. I didn't need to hide who I really was anymore. The whole world knew my identity, who I was and what I was trying to do.

And for the first time, in a twisted sort of irony, the world didn't fear me or the ULTRAs of the Resistance. Not anymore. Because they saw the truth now. It'd taken mass imprisonment by Saint's army of ULTRAbots—and his inner circle of defected ULTRAs—to make them realize, but finally they saw the truth.

Sometimes the grass isn't always greener on the other side.

But it wasn't humanity's fault. Humanity couldn't be blamed for its fear. They'd been manipulated by a man they thought was in power, Mr. Parsons. They'd been convinced the ULTRAs were the ones to fear, not the ULTRAbots.

Who could blame them?

What a pity they were so, so wrong.

I tasted metal on my tongue and realized I'd bitten my lip so hard that I was bleeding. I swallowed away the taste and kept on pressing. Kept on pushing. Saint couldn't get much further away. I was on to him. He might be stronger, but I was quicker. More agile. I could—

I smacked right into something when I made a teleportation leap.

I fell back. When I looked up, I saw five ULTRAbots above me. They looked tough. Tougher than any I'd encountered so far. Their weapons were bigger, and they seemed more agile than the usual ULTRAbots. Second models? Hell, who knew.

Didn't make a difference. I still had to take them down.

I flew into the one on the left, but it knocked me back before I could make contact. I kept my eye on Saint's dark cloud, gradually getting smaller. I needed to get to him. I needed to—

A fist crunched into my face.

The ULTRAbots above steadied their guns and went to fire.

I lifted my hands to stop the bullets. But the bullets were quick. Powerful. I tried to slow them down, to push them back, but I couldn't. They were too fast. Too strong.

In the corner of my eye, Saint got further away.

I bit down harder on my tongue, ignoring the taste of blood as best as I could. I stood my ground in the air. Pressed back on the bullets as they continued to fire from the ULTRAbots' guns. Harder. Harder...

And then I let go and teleported behind the ULTRAbots.

I took them down one by one.

But when I'd taken them down, I saw an explosion in the distance. Their bullets hit the side of a large hotel. Fire blasted from it. The glass all smashed, and the building started to fall.

As I stood there and looked at the chaos, I realized I'd made an error of judgment. I'd let my guard slip. All because of my perusal of Saint. All because I'd needed to catch him.

Saint.

I needed to stop him.

I needed to...

When I looked back, a bitter taste filled my mouth.

Saint was gone.

I was about to go after him in the direction he'd headed when I heard a shout in the distance. When I *felt* something bad inside. Now I don't know why this had started happening, but since I'd joined the Resistance, trained with them, I got this weird feeling when one of them was in danger. It was like we were all tapped into the same energy source. At first, I just put it down to me usually being anxious about some shit or other.

But I felt it now. I felt it, strong.

I teleported back to where the battle was unfolding above Manchester and saw exactly why I'd had a bad feeling.

Vortex was in the air.

She was surrounded by ULTRAbots.

And they were pulling their triggers.

[4]

I saw the ULTRAbots surround Vortex and fire their triggers and knew what I had to do.

I flew into their center. Teleported through them. I saw the bullets coming toward me then and knew I was going to be too late to stop all of them.

I focused my attention on a few of the bullets to the left. I slowed them down, then sped the bullets back at the ULTRAbots that'd fired them.

And then I felt the sharp, hot pain puncture the right side of my body and knew I was hit.

"Quick," I said. "Get—get out of here."

I saw Vortex looking at me with shock. She was looking at the right side of my body. I knew just from the look on her face that it wasn't good and that I must've taken some damage. I didn't want to look at it myself. Looking at wounds and blood just made me squeamish.

I turned to the rest of the ULTRAbots—the ones that'd fired at me—and I lifted my hand.

"You're gonna regret that," I said.

I fired a mass of ice into their bodies.

They froze right upon contact. One more hit and they'd be down completely. Shattered.

But I didn't have the strength in me right now to shatter them.

I dropped to the top of a nearby building, crouched down and leaned back against the wall at the side. I caught a glance at the side of my body. It made me feel sickly, made my toes curl. I'd taken a bad hit. I needed to heal myself. Fast.

I focused all my energy on that right side of my body. The healing process was never nice. It always stung. But I had to use it, or I wouldn't survive. If it weren't for my ability to heal, I'd die. I couldn't die. Not when Saint was still alive to kill.

I was in the middle of healing a puncture wound just underneath my ribcage when a group of ULTRAbots raised up at the side of the building right opposite me.

I looked them in the eye. They looked back at me. I kept my focus on that wound. Kept on healing it. I'd have to be quick, but I could still fight. I could...

When I saw who they had in their hands, my focus on healing slipped.

They were holding on to Ember. One of the ULTRAbots had a gun to his head. The ULTRAbot had a total dead look in its eyes, like it didn't care what it was doing, only that it had to carry it out.

I saw Ember struggling. Saw him trying to spark up the flames in his hands, but it was no use. The ULTRAbots had him. They'd got him right in their trap. There was no fighting back from Ember, not now.

I kept on healing that right side but I knew I didn't have long. Healing used up a lot of my powers, and when I'd finished healing, it always took a while for them to recharge to the max, too.

But I couldn't just sit here. I couldn't just watch something terrible happen to Ember.

"Hold still," I shouted, standing.

Ember didn't listen.

I lifted my hands. "Hold—"

The blast deafened me. It made me close my eyes. Hold my breath.

There was an explosion right beside Ember's head. An explosion from the ULTRAbot's gun.

Ember's head wasn't there anymore.

Neither was Ember.

I'd managed to form a wormhole around him just in time.

Now, Ember by my side, I fired ice at the ULTRAbots. I threw them aside using telekinesis. I re-routed their bullets through wormholes, threw them into one another, and I watched as Ember covered them in flames.

Together, we stood at the side of the building. I put my hands on my knees. The pain in my side was still bad. I'd used my powers way too soon after healing. I'd have to heal myself properly when we'd won this place.

"You okay?" I asked.

Ember shook his head. We didn't exactly get on like a house in... yeah, embers. Witty me. "No thanks to you."

"Hey. I just saved your ass."

"If you'd been here in the first place instead of chasing after shadows, you wouldn't've had to save my ass!"

I watched Ember walk to the side of the rooftop. Focused on healing myself. All around, up above, I saw the ULTRAbot numbers waning. The Resistance still stood strong. Manchester looked a little brighter all of a sudden.

I put my hand on Ember's back. "Looks like you did a good job."

When I heard the rumbling, humming sound behind me, I realized I might just've spoken too soon.

I looked back. Saw exactly what I'd feared but exactly what I'd expected.

More ULTRAbots. A thick wall of them, moving in a spherical mass. More than we'd fought here. More than we could deal with.

The Resistance floated by my side.

"What do we do?" Ember asked.

I looked at Orion. Although I couldn't see his eyes underneath his black mask, I knew he wasn't happy. He had that demeanor he always had when he was pissed with me. "We do the only thing we can do," he said. "We run."

I shook my head. Many of the others in the Resistance groaned and cursed. "We don't have to give up," I said.

"Yes we do," Orion said. "There's more than we can handle. Way more than we can handle. Maybe if we'd dealt with the first wave in time, we could've prevented a second wave from following."

"You don't know that."

"We had a chance, Kyle. We could've stopped this. We could've traced down their production facility. We could've prevented this, if we'd all been here to prevent it."

I heard the disappointment in Orion's voice. I felt it, too. Felt it from all the ULTRAs around me. I knew what they were disappointed about. I knew what they were hinting at. This was my fault. I'd gone after Saint, so this was my fault.

"So what about Manchester?" Roadrunner asked.

Orion took a few seconds to answer as he stared at the oncoming mass of ULTRAbots.

Then, he finally spoke the words that none of us wanted to hear.

"Manchester is lost."

5

"You were irresponsible and you know you were irresponsible. At least be responsible enough to recognize and accept that much."

I listened to Orion's voice droning on and I wanted to be anywhere but here right now.

It was night. We were on an island in the middle of the Pacific. The island was so small that it was pretty much nameless, but the Resistance had taken to it since the rest of the world was pretty much a no-go zone. It was a good place to have. A safe place, which got absolutely boiling in the day. Even Vortex had managed to catch herself a bit of a tan.

But when Saint was out there raining chaos on the world, I couldn't help feeling I was wasting my time here.

"I did what I had to do," I said.

"You could've got Vortex killed."

"But I didn't."

"You could've got Ember—"

"But I didn't."

Orion sighed. He turned away and looked out to sea. As much as I got frustrated being stuck on this island, the sea calmed me. I saw the ripples in the water, the moon shimmering across its surface. All around, total silence. Peace. I wanted peace for the whole world again. I wished there were more places like this. More places where what was left of the un-prisoned humanity could go. But I knew we were running out of territory, and soon, the Resistance wouldn't even have this place to call home.

Saint and his ULTRAbots would find us, eventually.

And when they did... I just hoped we'd be ready for them.

Orion lit a fire in the sticks in front of him with the wave of a hand. "You know, you're strong. You're powerful."

"I know that much."

"And I respect that you're only trying to fight Saint, just like I did," Orion continued, ignoring me. "But there are stages to a battle. Stages to every battle, especially one on this scale. You don't start the battle by taking down the hardest source. You start small. And then you work your way up the scale with smaller victories until eventually, the hardest source isn't even hard at all. It's nothing but soft. And then..."

"And then you kill him," I said.

Orion sighed. "You're driven by too much hatred."

"Hatred is what makes us powerful."

"No. No, that's where you're wrong. And you know you're wrong. *Love* makes us far more powerful than anger ever can. Forgiveness burns a much brighter light than the black void of vengeance."

I bit my lip. "So that's why you didn't kill Saint? That's why you didn't save the world? Because forgiveness burns a brighter light?"

Orion hesitated. I could sense the discomfort he felt about the question. "I put Saint somewhere I thought he could never come back from. I made an error of judgment."

"So you regret not killing him?"

"No."

"So what happened to my family. What happened to my sister and my mom. What's happened to the whole damned world. If you could go back and kill him, you're seriously saying you wouldn't?"

My anger was at a peak. I could feel my powers on edge. I wanted to hurt something. Someone. I wanted to make the people responsible for my loss go through hell for what they'd done to the people I loved.

"What happened to the world is unfortunate."

"Too damned right it's unfortunate."

"But I stand by my morals. We do not kill our own. It does not matter whether we love them or hate them. We do not kill our own."

"Pity Saint didn't share those morals when he killed Slice and Aqua."

I knew it was a low blow, but I needed one right now. I knew it'd hurt Orion, bringing up Slice and Aqua, who'd died at the hands of Saint when he'd first returned. I was basically blaming Orion for what'd happened to them, and I got that wasn't so cool.

But Orion didn't react with anger. He didn't react with frustration. "I made a decision not to kill Saint. I cannot be held accountable for Saint's anger. If a prisoner is put in a cell and that prisoner escapes and goes on to kill, can the person who locked him away in hope of reformation be put to blame? Or should the prisoner not have been given a second chance at all? Should he have received the death penalty?"

I shook my head and stood. "I can't talk about this right now."

"But when we, together, have an opportunity—a responsibility—to fight for a falling city, we take that opportunity. We live up to our potential. We don't go chasing phantoms into the clouds."

I turned around, gobsmacked. "Okay, so what you're saying is it's okay when *you* make a pig's ass of things, but when *I* make a mistake, the entire fall of a city's on me?"

Orion didn't nod. He didn't shake his head. He just gave me that look like there was a difference in the things we'd done.

I waved my hand at him and walked away. I needed to get deep into the rainforest. I needed to be alone. I needed to think.

"Forgiveness is a far, far stronger power than vengeance will ever be, Kyle. Don't you ever forget that. Don't you ever forget who you are."

I tensed my fists and felt them cover with ice.

I disappeared into the forest, Orion's words fading into the distance, and I plotted my next move against Saint.

Because I was going to make him pay, whether Orion liked it or not.

I hadn't forgotten myself. I remembered myself well. I remembered my sister who'd died. I remembered my mom who'd died. I remembered all the people who'd fallen at the hands of Saint.

I knew who I was. I knew *exactly* who I was.

And I wasn't ever giving up until I looked Saint in the eye and took his life.

6

I flew over the island and knew damned well I should be far, far away from here.

It was night. There was warmth to the air, though. Humidity, which I longed to sit in, longed to be a part of. Sure, I'd never been all that good in the heat—I hated how stuffy it made me feel. But since embracing my responsibilities as an ULTRA; since shedding the dual identities I'd worked so hard to maintain, I longed for a break, more than anything.

And a break with the people I loved most in the world was absolutely at the top of my list.

Below, on the quaint island, I saw little flickers of lights inside the small houses. In the distance, the waves crashed gently against the shore. I knew that down there, I'd find my family. I'd find Dad, and my friends, Damon, and Avi, and their families.

And I'd find Ellicia.

I moved down slowly toward the island. I shouldn't be here, that was for sure. But I felt like I needed their guidance right now. I felt like I needed them to ground me. To tell me what was right and what was wrong; to steer my path.

But at the same time, I knew just by being here, I was putting them in danger. I'd chosen this island for them to stay while the chaos between Saint and us went down not just 'cause I'd saved this island once before, but because of how secluded and out of the way it was.

I knew, chances were, that it'd fall one day. It'd fall just like the rest of the world.

But I was hoping Saint would be dealt with by the time that day came around.

I drifted further down toward the houses. Landed on the sandy ground. Now I was on the ground, I could feel a slight cool breeze, which carried with it the faint smell of cooking meat. I imagined sitting around a barbecue with Ellicia, Damon, and Avi, and my dad. I imagined us all sitting around and laughing, not a care in the world.

I hoped that day would come. I really did. But it seemed so distant. So far away. So impossible.

I lifted off the ground again and hovered nearer to the houses, being sure to keep my invisibility activated. I was still stinging a bit on my right side from where I'd been hit by bullets in the battle for Manchester. That'd fade, though. It always did, in time.

Plus, I knew it was only right that I felt some pain for my part in the loss of that battle.

I moved past the houses and peeked through the little windows. I saw families gathered around fires. I saw parents reading to children. I saw happiness. I saw peace. I couldn't believe I was actually in the same world as the one I'd fought the battle in not long ago. That was the thing about Saint's rule. One day, you could wake up feeling like your city, your island, your country was the safest place in the world. The next thing you know, you're trapped. Imprisoned.

Nobody knew why Saint was doing what he was doing. He

wanted total rule, sure. But he didn't seem to be killing any of the humans. Unlike Nycto, whose goal was to wipe humanity out due to his little-boy-got-bullied issues, Saint enjoyed the idea of total rule. Total control.

That was the thing. He *liked* humans.

Only problem was, he liked them when they were working for him; when they gave him the ultimate ego boost.

I was about to turn the corner to the next house when I heard a voice behind me.

I felt my skin soften. Felt my muscles weaken. Good job it was dark because for a moment, I swear my invisibility slipped.

I looked around and saw Ellicia and Damon walking together.

Ellicia looked even more beautiful every time I saw her. Again, it was dark, so I couldn't see her properly. I didn't have to. I could imagine her long, dark hair. I could smell that strawberry flavor from the shampoo she used to use. I could feel her lips against mine, her warmth against my body as we cuddled, like I was reliving those moments all over again.

Damon was the same, too. Well, not the same as Ellicia, but the same as he always was. Tall. Bulky. Walked clumsily and spoke a little loudly.

I stepped to one side and held on to my invisibility as they passed.

"I just wonder if he's ever coming back," Ellicia said.

Damon's feet scraped against the ground. They stopped just outside a house. "He will come back. Man, I'd love to say I know Kyle, but I dunno if I do anymore. Not after all this Glacies business. But if there's one thing for sure, he's a fighter. He ain't gonna lay down and let Saint take this world."

"How can you be so sure?"

I waited. Waited for Damon to answer. I wanted to step in.

To tell them both I was here. That I was back, and the war was being won.

But that would be lying.

The Resistance weren't winning the war at all.

Damon put a hand on Ellicia's arm. Even though it was clear he was only being friendly, I couldn't help the glimmer of jealousy I felt inside. I wanted to be the one there comforting her. I wanted to be the one to tell her everything was gonna be okay.

"I'm sure because I've seen what he can do. We've both seen what he can do. And we've gotta believe that if he keeps on doing what we know he can do, things will get back to the way they were."

"They'll never be the way they were. Not for us. Not for... not for Kyle."

I felt my muscles loosen. With the sad way Ellicia spoke, it made me think of Mom, and the others I'd lost.

"But they'll be better again," Damon said. "Anyway. I should probably get some sleep."

"Yeah. Sure."

"Avi's lent me that dating guide."

"The one with—"

"4.4 on Goodreads, yeah. Or it might be 4.3 now. Is Goodreads even still a thing now?"

"I don't..."

"Can't imagine Saint cracking down on book-related social media, can you?"

Ellicia giggled. And again, as much as I loved the pair of them, I wanted to be the one cheering her up. Making her laugh.

"Night, Ellicia," Damon said.

She nodded. Smiled. "Goodnight."

I watched as Damon waddled off toward his home. And as I

hovered there, totally invisible, I realized it was just me and Ellicia then. Me and Ellicia standing there in the dark. Both of us opposite one another. Staring at one another.

She was so close that I could reach out and stroke her hair. So close that I could lean into her ear and tell her everything was going to be okay.

She stared through me a little longer, then she sighed, and turned around, into her house.

I listened to the door close and I let my invisibility drop.

Then as the lights flickered off in her house, I held my breath and disappeared.

7

Saint looked over the map of conquered territory and he smiled.

It was two a.m., but it could've been any time at all. He didn't go outside much these days. He didn't need to, not since his tower had been erected. A mile long structure shooting right into the sky from the middle of the Atlantic, towering over everyone. It could be seen from miles away.

And that's what he wanted. He wanted people to know he was there. He wanted everyone to know he was watching.

He stood in his office and listened to the droning sounds of work beneath him. Not only were ULTRAbots being produced at a rapid rate, but they had other experiments going on, too. Things to prepare for. And things he was working on. Things he was very excited about.

He looked at the date. January 14th. He'd targeted the 1st for the launch of his new project, but some unfortunate errors had crept into their well-oiled ship. But that didn't matter in the grand scheme of things. A few days were insignificant.

What mattered was what was coming.

"Saint?"

Saint turned around and saw Controlla looking at him. Controlla was a lanky guy with longish, dark hair. He'd originally sided with that lame imitator, Nycto, but after Saint had launched his attack, he was one of the ULTRAs to join Saint's cause in the takeover of humanity, the fight against the Resistance. He was useful. He could get inside minds and change the will of any individual. A very raw power, but one that fascinated Saint. He'd be a handy ally, until Saint needed him no more.

Saint smiled. His helmet suffocated his face, but he was used to the sensation by now. It made him feel powerful. At ease. "Good news, I hope?"

Saint didn't even have to say those words. He could tell by the look on Controlla's face that it was a combination of good and bad news.

"A bit of both," Controlla said, in that Scottish accent of his; an accent Saint couldn't help admiring.

"Let's start with the good news. Then we'll see whether I'm in the mood for discouragement."

Controlla's glance broke away. "The—the good news is, we took Manchester and Liverpool. We've got total control of England."

Saint's smile widened. He already knew this, but he liked to stay coy about the full extent of his powers. He liked the element of surprise it offered him over others. "That's excellent."

"It leaves us with just a little territory left to conquer. Mostly the Pacific islands."

Saint's smile widened even more. "Indeed it does."

He knew for a fact that the Resistance had a base somewhere in the Pacific. He didn't know where exactly, but he knew that soon enough, he'd find it. And when he did, he'd destroy it.

He wouldn't kill the remnants of the Resistance. Not at all. In fact, he had a much more intriguing fate in mind for them.

All that linked to the next stage of his plan.

Of course, you could be forgiven for thinking it was a coincidence that the Pacific was the last remaining place in the world left to conquer; the place where the Resistance just so happened to be. But that was all part of the plan, too. There was a reason Saint wanted them last. Partly because he wanted to watch their hope and resolve fade, slowly.

And then he wanted them to have front row seats to the dawn of a new world.

"And the bad news?" Saint asked.

Again, Controlla lowered his head.

"Don't look so sheepish. The good news is *very* good. It'll take a lot to topple it."

Controlla half-glanced up at Saint. Saint knew why he was so hesitant. He'd heard the rumors, no doubt. The rumors of what Saint did to the ULTRAs who upset him. Of how worthless they were to him now his ULTRAbot program was in full swing.

The new world order was so close he could taste it in the air.

"There's someone here," Controlla said. "He fought through the gates and worked his way up here."

Saint's top lip twitched. "How?"

"We're not sure. But he's... he's powerful. And he said he wants to see you. Said he'll die trying to see you if he has to."

Saint weighed up his options. His gates were impenetrable. Whoever was here had to be strong. Very strong. "Where is he?"

"He's just outside."

"With guards?"

Controlla nodded. "But he insists he isn't here for any harm."

Saint paused. Who had the gall to confront him? Who had

the sheer stupidity to walk into his home and demand a meeting with him? "Said he'll die trying, did he?"

"Mhm."

"Good job," Saint said, walking toward the door. "At least he's prepared for what's..."

The words slipped away when he approached the door. He'd been expecting someone powerful, but not him. He thought he was gone. Thought he was dead. And that was a misjudgment, sure. An error of the moment that if he could turn back the clock, he would've prevented.

But he didn't have to. Because *he* was still alive.

"I'm here because I want to help you. Help you take down the Resistance. Help you take the rest of the planet."

Saint looked at the ULTRAbots surrounding this person.

He looked at the silver clothing of the boy opposite. Gosh, was it such a lame imitation of his own. He looked at the desperate look in his tired eyes.

This wasn't bad news. This wasn't bad news at all.

"Nycto," Saint said. "How nice to see you again."

8

Six hours solid training with the Resistance and already Vortex had screwed with my mind a ton of times already.

The afternoon sun was scalding hot, making sweat drip down the back of my neck no matter how much I tried to cool myself down with my handy icy powers. The island looked beautiful, in all truth. Amazing to believe how different the world could be in a matter of miles—snow in New York, blazing sunlight and luscious greens in the Pacific islands. I looked at the blue sea, felt the warm sand between my toes and wanted nothing more than to throw myself in that water. Sure, water still freaked me out after some weird memory I had of being nearly drowned as a kid—memories I still couldn't get my head round. But you get the idea. It was lush weather. I wanted to make the most of it.

Instead, Vortex was testing my "resistance."

"I'd appreciate it if you held off with the flying frogs," I said, putting my hands on my knees.

Vortex smiled. Even she seemed to be catching some sun. Just a little. "You like them?"

"Not really. I mean, I don't think they're funny."

"They're not supposed to be funny, Kyle."

"Well they're not scary, either."

"You seem pretty touchy about them."

"That's because I don't like being pasted with flying frogs. How's that supposed to test my resistance?"

"You're punching them across the ocean at full strength, right?"

"Well, I guess I..."

"Then they're testing your strength." She looked at me like it was just common sense then smiled.

I lifted my fists again. Held my ground. "Go on then. Give me some more."

The second I spoke, the entire island went pitch black. I felt a shiver run up my spine. All around, I heard groans—the groans that sounded like they came from zombies in the wacky old horror films.

When I turned around, I realized that's because they were exactly that. Zombies.

They were wading toward me through the sand. I could smell their rotting flesh, taste it on my lips. Some of them had arms missing. Others had holes in their legs.

Their teeth snapped together, echoing through the silence.

As much as I knew they were just creations of the mind—or rather, creations of Vortex's mind to test my resistance—I couldn't help feeling a little afraid of these zombies. I'd always been scared of them ever since I'd read some zombie books by a British guy. Dead Days, or something. Enough to give anyone the creeps.

I stood my ground and fired a bolt of ice at the first of the zombies.

But something weird happened.

No ice fired out.

I went to fire again and realized I couldn't. I was standing there, completely naked. I felt exposed. Totally exposed.

I looked up at the groaning zombies. They were just inches away from me, clawing out at my skin.

"So no ice," I muttered. "No damned ice. Cheers, Vortex. I'll just have to..."

I went to throw a boatload of telekinesis at the zombies and realized that wasn't working either.

The zombie grabbed my arm. Dragged it to its mouth.

I punched it away, suddenly feeling like this whole scenario was very real, and fell back onto the sand. When I looked up, I saw all the zombies surrounding me, getting ready to feast.

I clambered to my feet and ran. Ran across the sand. I felt slow, though. Slower than I'd felt in a long time. I was exhausted. I wasn't sure how much energy I had in me.

I just knew I had to run.

I kept on wading through the sand but it stretched up my legs. I was sinking. Sinking into the ground and there was nothing I could do about it. Nothing at all.

When I looked back to check how far away the zombies were, I froze.

Mike Beacon's zombified figure stood opposite me.

Beside him, Cassie.

And beside her, Mom.

They all closed in on me. I felt tears roll down my cheeks. This wasn't right. This was too hard. Too damned hard, even by Vortex's standards.

"Help!" I tried to claw my way from the sand. Banged my hands against it as I sank further and further, as the trio of people I'd lost reached down for my head.

"Help!" I screamed at the top of my voice.

Their hands grabbed my head.

"It's okay. It's okay—"

"Get off me!"

"Kyle, it's okay."

I saw then I was looking into Vortex's eyes. She was holding my arms. I was on the beach in the sunlight again. In the distance, I saw more of the Resistance looking at me like I was weird.

I backed away, still shaky. I noticed I'd been crying in real life, too. "What the hell was that?"

"Kyle, I don't—"

"You know damn well what you did just then."

"I swear, I didn't... I lost control. Lost control of everything. I dunno what happened."

"Yeah right. Like this wasn't some kind of revenge."

"Revenge?"

"For what happened in Manchester."

Vortex's cheeks blushed a little. I was shouting and making quite a scene. "You saved me in Manchester. Sure, you put me in a bad situation in the first place, but you saved me. I don't want any revenge for that. I forgive you."

I was the one blushing now. I rubbed my hand against the back of my neck. "Then—then what happened right then. What was it? How did it..."

I saw Vortex's eyes roll back into her head, like she was slipping into one of her trances.

But something weird happened.

She shot into the air. Shot upwards, right above the island.

I squinted up into the sunlight. I didn't know what she was doing, where she was going. Only that something was wrong. Very wrong.

Then I saw the second figure.

The sun bounced off their chest in a way that told me who it was. I didn't even have to see their face to know.

And then I felt that urge for revenge fill my body once again.

Saint was here.

Saint had Vortex.

But he wasn't going to get away. Not this time.

9

I saw Saint taking Vortex away and I didn't have to think about what I was going to do.

I fired after him. Flew up into the blue sky as fast as I possibly could. The island disappeared beneath my feet as I got higher and higher, as the air whooshed past my ears and my lips dried with the force.

I felt my hands cover with ice. Saint had taken enough from me. He'd done enough damage to the Resistance, and to the world in general. I wasn't letting him take Vortex.

I was making him pay.

I wondered if any of the other Resistance members had seen what I'd seen. It seemed weird they weren't joining me. As much as Orion grilled me for my "obsession" with vengeance against Saint, he'd still defend the members of the Resistance if Saint arrived at our doorstep, right?

Not just that, but Saint was at the island, which meant he knew where I was. What was stopping him hopping over a few more islands and finding everyone I'd ever cared about?

I teleported myself closer toward the glimmer of light.

I stopped when I saw Vortex right in front of me.

She was still. Completely still, hovering in the air. Her eyes weren't rolled back into her head, which meant she wasn't in one of her dream-inducing trances. But there was something about her. Something... off about the way she looked at me. Like she didn't totally recognize me.

"Vortex?" I wondered whether this could just be another part of her resistance training. Maybe she'd gone into a trance. Maybe the whole thing with the imaginary zombies, with me waking up from it, maybe it was all part of the training. Perhaps I hadn't really woken up. Perhaps this was just another layer to the challenge.

But I wasn't sure. This felt very real.

"Saint," I said, looking all around. I couldn't see him anywhere. "Did you see where he went?"

"Saint's right here," she said.

It took me a second to clock what Vortex said. "What do—"

She flew into my chest and knocked me out of the sky.

I fell rapidly down to the island, the wind knocked out of my gut. Vortex had hit me. She'd hit me and she'd said, "Saint's right here". This couldn't be real. This had to be some kind of trance. What did any of it mean?

I readjusted my balance when Vortex flew into me again.

"Vortex, what—"

She punched me in the back of the neck. Hard. And then she pulled back my arms as I tried to swing them at her and kicked me away. I didn't want to fight her. After all, this was Vortex. She was strong, but I knew my powers were much stronger. Among the strongest in the world.

I could feel someone trying to get into my mind. A feeling I couldn't explain. I held my ground, resisted it, and stood tall as Vortex flew at me once more.

I dodged her attack. Appeared behind her.

"What the hell is this?"

She swung for me, so I teleported to her side again. I was still winded, but I had enough energy in me to keep on dodging around her, to keep on resisting her attacks.

I didn't want to fight back. I *couldn't* fight back. But Vortex wasn't leaving me much of a choice right now.

I fired ice at her fists as she flew toward me. It didn't stop her, though. She kept on going until the ice cracked into my chest and knocked me back.

I fell backward. Wobbled through the air. I tasted blood on my lips. "Vortex, what the hell is this?"

I saw Vortex was looking at me then with fear. With confusion. And I saw that she wasn't in control of her actions right now. Someone else was. Someone was using her to fight against me. Someone was...

I saw the glimmer of silver in the corner of my eye again.

I was torn. Torn between staying here with Vortex, helping her get out of this state.

But Saint.

The glimmer of light. It was Saint. It had to be Saint. He was doing this.

He wasn't going to get away with it.

Screw what Orion said about starting small. If I was cutting away any part of the snake, it was the head—

A crack against my jaw, then my mind went dizzy.

I fell. And as I fell, I saw that glimmer of silver disappear. He'd gone. Saint had gone all over again.

"You let him get away!" I shouted.

I flew at Vortex this time and didn't hold back. I rammed her backward. Fired ice at her hands as she kept on swinging, kept on punching. I knew what I was doing was wrong. I knew she couldn't be in control of herself.

But she'd punched me. She'd got in my way when I was trying to stop Saint. We'd failed to catch him all over again.

I kept on fighting Vortex. And soon, I became aware of just how high we were. We were well above the clouds. The purple glow of space was just inches away. Soon, Vortex wouldn't be able to breathe. I would—I was special like that. But if I stayed up here much longer, Vortex was going to die.

I grabbed her. Resisted all her attacks. It was weird that she hadn't just used her mind tricks on me. Whoever was controlling her must not be able to tap into those.

I dragged her back down to earth, through the icy clouds.

She kept on fighting back.

"Come on," I said. "We're almost there. We're almost—"

"You've made a big mistake," she said.

I looked at her then. I didn't know what she meant. "What do..."

Then I heard the explosion.

The explosion down by the island.

On the island.

The Resistance's island was under attack, and I was right up here in the clouds.

10

I heard the explosion down on the island and felt sickening guilt spread through my body.

I squinted down, the sunlight blinding me. The thickening clouds were in the way, too. Those clouds made me feel uneasy simply because I associated clouds with Saint. I just hoped he wasn't here right now, after all. He'd flown away. He'd disappeared into the sky.

But what was stopping him just appearing down by the island now he'd lured me away?

What was stopping him using powers I knew damned well he had?

I felt something hit my back. A winding punch that knocked the breath from my lungs. I turned around and saw Vortex still hovering there. She had that recognizable look on her face, a familiarity about her. But it was clear she wasn't in control of her actions, not totally.

"I'm sorry," I said. "There's... there's somewhere I have to be right now."

As Vortex flew in for another punch, I teleported myself down toward the island.

The moment I tried to teleport, a splitting headache cracked through my skull. I heard buzzing, like the static on a television turned up too loud. Bitter smells filled my mouth, and the taste of sick hung to the back of my throat.

I couldn't teleport. Something was stopping me from teleporting. Dampening my powers.

I held my breath and tried to disappear again.

That static sound. The taste of sick. Flashes in my vision.

"You need to learn when you're defeated," a voice said.

I wasn't sure where it came from. I looked all around. It wasn't Vortex. And it didn't look like there was anyone else here.

I tried to shoot down but felt my body lift up into the air instead.

I bit down on my bottom lip, hard. I couldn't explain what was happening, couldn't understand it. It felt like I was losing my grip on my own mind. When I saw Vortex acting the way she was, I wondered whether whoever was doing that to her was doing it to me, too. Trying to worm their way into my head. Control me.

"Just give up, Glacies. Give up and hand yourself over. There doesn't have to be any more bloodshed."

I could hear the voice loud and clear in my mind now. So much so that I was convinced of what was happening—some kind of mind-controller was trying to take over my thoughts.

I heard more explosions below. Saw flashes of light between the clouds. The island of the Resistance. It was under attack.

My muscles tightened. My thoughts drifted. Maybe I could just stay up here and watch...

"Yes. Stay up here and watch."

Maybe I could just—

"No!"

I shook my head. Held my breath. I focused on my body.

Tensed my fists. I wasn't giving up on the island. I wasn't giving up on my people. My ULTRAs.

I flew back down. It felt like I was running through mud. I wondered about Vortex. She wasn't chasing me anymore. I wasn't sure why, but it could only be a good thing, I guess.

I kept on flying down, battling the magnetic force pulling me back, telling me to turn around.

"You don't have to fight."

"I have to fight," I muttered.

"You can stand and watch as your island falls—"

"I have to fight!"

I used a massive burst of energy to blast through the clouds.

When I saw what was on the other side of them, I almost lost my mind all over again.

The island was burning. Mini-explosions were erupting everywhere. The Resistance were fleeing. Trying to hide. Trying to...

Wait.

I flew closer to the island. I definitely didn't feel strong enough to teleport, so flying had to suffice for now. As specks of warm rain fell from the clouds around me, I saw it wasn't the Resistance fleeing at all.

It was the Resistance attacking the island.

I saw Stone smashing up our homes.

I saw Roadrunner sprinting around, throwing her body and bashing through things.

I saw Ember setting things alight.

And I saw Orion, hovering over, big powerful balls of energy in the palms of his hands, and getting ready to fire.

"No!"

I flew toward Orion. I couldn't let him destroy the island. I couldn't let any of this happen—whatever the hell was even happening at all.

When I flew at him, I saw Orion turn around. Look right at me.

There was fear in his eyes. Fear and a lack of understanding. A look of sheer confusion.

"Go," Orion said. "Just—just go."

I held my ground. Shook my head. "I'm not going anywhere. I'm not letting this island fall."

Within an instant, Orion wasn't alone.

Stone was beside him. Roadrunner was beside him. Ember and Vortex and the rest of the Resistance, all of them were beside him.

Their powers were charged up.

They were looking right at me, some with fear in their eyes, others with confusion. Others devoid of emotion completely.

"Go!" Orion shouted.

I didn't go.

I didn't have a chance to.

The Resistance all lifted their hands and fired their powers right at me.

11

I threw myself out of the way of the collective blast from every single Resistance member.

I saw the beams of power racing toward me. Flames. Water. Electricity. They filled the sky, made the air around me rumble. I couldn't see the ULTRAs—the ULTRAs that were clearly under the control of something or someone—behind the energy.

I just tried to fly away from them, to teleport away from the blasts of energy.

But I still wasn't strong enough to teleport.

I gritted my teeth and watched as the energy surrounded me. I could heal from some things, sure. But hundreds of the most powerful blasts of energy imaginable? Yeah. I didn't fancy picking up the pieces of my body when it covered the island.

I stuck out my hands, as much as the magnetic force behind me tried to pull me back. I wasn't being controlled by this bastard. I was strong enough to hold my ground. Strong enough to fight.

I saw the energy getting closer and focused on all my anger. I focused on Saint, and the revenge I wanted to take out on him.

I focused on Ellicia. On Damon. On the people I was fighting for, all along.

I focused on my sister.

My mom.

I squeezed my eyes shut. The beams of energy were so close that I could feel their power just inches from my face.

I held my position. Threw everything I had back at that energy.

And then I felt a loosening in the air.

I didn't want to open my eyes. I didn't want to see what'd happened just in case it wasn't something I wanted to look at.

But I did. And when I looked, I saw the energy wasn't in front of me anymore.

It was drifting upwards. All of the streams of fire, the beams of electricity, all of them were rising up into the sky, controlled by me.

I looked at the Resistance, at the people I cared about. For a split second, I wondered if I'd have to get rid of them. I didn't want to. They were my people; my family. But if they were fighting me, trying to take me down, then what was I supposed to do?

I threw the energy beams up into the sky, right past the clouds and out of the Earth's atmosphere.

Then I teleported behind the Resistance and shot around the island.

I could feel it, now. Feel the presence of someone trying to control me. The same person—ULTRA—controlling everyone else. Behind, I heard the whooshing of my fellow ULTRAs pursuing me. I watched more power fire past me, some of it singeing my flesh as it scratched my face, my torso.

But I was getting closer to whoever was doing this. I was going to stop them.

I could feel an energy coming from the very middle of the

island. A transmission, almost, reaching out to me and to the rest of the Resistance, making them fight me. I flew toward it. Teleported, now I had my strength back. It still hurt. There was still some kind of static sound, and I figured this ULTRA must have some kind of block set up. Something stopping me using my full abilities.

It wasn't going to stop me for long.

I stormed past the trees and appeared right in the middle of the island. When I got there, I saw a waterfall. I saw tropical birds flying around.

Up above, I saw a guy.

He was young. Probably my age, maybe a little older. He was dressed all in dark red. His eyes shone.

When he looked at me, I felt like he was speaking to me. Like he was looking around my mind for a weakness, trying to get a grip on me.

"It's over," I shouted.

The guy tilted his head. Smiled. "Really? I thought we were just getting started."

He shot up into the sky and vanished into the clouds.

But not for long.

I teleported in front of him, as much as it weakened me. I grabbed him. Held him there, in the middle of the clouds. Underneath us, I could hear the mass of controlled ULTRAs from the Resistance closing in.

I squeezed this guy's shoulders and looked deeper into his eyes. "Your party trick. Controlling minds. It's good, but it's not all there just yet."

I tried to teleport the pair of us away, but the resistance to teleportation was so strong that I almost lost my grip on this guy.

He smiled. Laughed. His teeth were bright white. "That's why they call me Controlla."

"Controlla?" I said. "Seriously? Like the—"

"Drake song. Yeah. Why, is that a bad thing?"

"No. No, I kind of liked that song. It's just... I dunno. What next? 'Hotline Bling'?"

"You haven't met 'Hotline Bling' yet?"

"You serious?"

Controlla shook his head. "No. I'm just kidding. Anyway. Where were we?"

He punched me in the back so hard that I went flying face flat down into the water below.

I lashed free of it. Memories of a blurry past crowded my mind. I'd been underwater. Someone had held me under there. I felt like that was the day where my powers sparked, but I still couldn't totally explain what had happened.

The weird thing about the memory?

I had a funny feeling, now more than ever, that there were two more people being dunked in the water beside me.

Their little fingertips touching mine.

I dragged myself out of the water. Wiped the water from my eyes and gasped for breath. I had to catch Controlla. Stop his grip on my friends. Stop him—

"Don't move a muscle, Kyle."

My stomach sank.

I turned around and saw Stone standing right opposite me.

Even though his eyes told me he wanted to do anything but fight, his arms were totally covered in rock.

He was ready to fight.

12

I looked at Stone as he tensed his solid rock fists and really, really hoped I didn't have to fight someone so close to me.

He walked to me. The sounds of the falling waterfall filled the silence. My head ached, hard, and I couldn't shake the taste of blood from my lips. I was exhausted. Completely out of breath, completely beaten down. I wasn't sure how much further I could go.

"Stone, please—"

"You've seen what's happening to this island. So now it's time to join us. Or die."

I shook my head as Stone walked closer. I knew I could fight him if I had to. Sure, he was strong, but I was stronger. Then again, that scared me. I didn't want to have to use my strength against Stone. He was a part of the inner circle. He'd accepted me into the Resistance despite so much of my bullshit in the early days. "Stone, this isn't you. You can fight this. You're strong enough to fight this."

Stone stepped right up to me. He stopped. Looked me in the eye. For a split second, as the flames appeared all around us in the burning forest, I saw life in Stone's eyes. I saw a spark of realization. Of him remembering who he was.

I reached out a hand to him. Put it on his arm. "It's me. It's Kyle. Glacies. And you're a part of the Resistance. You're being controlled by some little douchebag called Controlla. That's right. Someone who names himself after Drake songs. But you don't have to be. Not—"

Stone's fist cracked into my face.

I felt my jaw dislodge. More blood filled my mouth. I fell back and hit the ground, more stunned that Stone had actually punched me than anything. I felt specks of warm rain drizzling down as the weather made another turn. My head spun. I wasn't sure how much fight I had in me.

"Please," I said, regretting it right away as my dangling jaw wobbled out of place. "Don't—"

Stone kicked me back.

I went flying into the waterfall. Splashed through it and crashed into the rocks behind it. I tried to heal myself, but I couldn't. I tried to get myself away from here, but I couldn't.

I knew what I had to do.

I had to fight Stone, as much as I didn't want to.

He appeared right at the mouth of the waterfall. He stepped up to me, his rocky feet echoing against the solid walls of this cavern. His fists tightened and the rock solidified even harder. "You just don't know when to stop fighting, do you?"

I cracked my jaw back into place. It was agony, and it wasn't a full heal, but it'd do for now. "I won't stop fighting. Not while Saint's minions are controlling you."

He rushed over toward me and punched me heavily, right in my gut.

"You're going to fall," Stone said. It was his voice, but I knew he wasn't really talking. He wouldn't say words like this. "You're going to fall, and so too is everything around you. It's going to crumble."

He hit the back of the rock wall.

I felt rocks tumble down around me.

"I won't fall because I'll keep fighting," I said, looking Stone in the eyes now. "I'll keep on fighting *you* and I'll keep on fighting Saint until you're—"

Another punch to the gut.

More rocks fell beside me.

I looked back up at Stone. His eyes had completely glazed over. I didn't recognize him. Didn't recognize anything of the Stone I used to know. And as he pulled back his fist for another punch, the anger built up inside me.

I didn't see Stone. I saw Saint.

And I knew what I had to do to Saint.

"You're weak," Stone said. "Weaker than you think you are."

"How'd you figure that one out?"

Stone smiled. It looked forced. "You just are. You're driven so much by hate that you don't see the damage it's doing."

"If it puts a stop to Saint, then it's working just fine."

"Let's see if you're still saying that when I put your friends through hell."

I couldn't resist the urge to fight back then. The mention of my friends tipped me over the edge, even if I was well aware that it wasn't Stone swinging the punches at all.

I grabbed his wrist. Put all that anger and focus on holding it in midair. "Bad idea," I said.

Then I fired the pair of us out of the waterfall and down into the water.

I held my breath as I was submerged. Stone tried to hit back at me, but I kept on pushing him further and further down. I saw red. I didn't see Stone. Just Saint. Saint and his minions, like Controlla. The people who'd torn my life apart; who were tearing the whole planet apart.

I couldn't forgive.

I couldn't forget.

I had to stop him, even if it meant taking Stone down.

I squeezed my hands around his neck, the power inside me getting stronger. I saw the life return to his eyes. Saw the look of Stone return. I heard him gurgling under the water. Saw him grab my wrists, try to bend them away. But we kept on descending. I kept on pushing him down.

And as we descended further, for a moment, I felt like everything was going to be okay. Like I was going to make Saint pay for what he'd done. And this was just the start of that. This was just the very start.

Stone's mouth moved in the shape of my name. "Kyle! Kyle!" he silently shouted under the water. I noticed the rocks from his hands had gone. He was just a person. Just a person who I was holding underwater, pushing them to their death.

He patted my hand and I saw the life disappear from his eyes.

I saw them glaze over completely.

In that instant, I saw what I'd done. Exactly what I'd done.

And it horrified me.

I dragged Stone out of the water. Put him down by the waterside.

"Stone!" I crouched beside him. Pressed my hands on his body. Fired air into his lungs. "Stone, please!"

But Stone was completely still.

I pressed my head against his chest and punched it, hard. I banged my fists against it, hoping the water would spout up from his lips.

But still, nothing happened.

I leaned back and felt the horror of what I'd done. The horror that blind vengeance could bring.

"You little shit."

I looked down and saw Stone's eyes were open.

His fists were tensed.

He punched me in the side of the head and knocked the consciousness out of me.

The last thought I had as I drifted into blackness?

I probably deserved that punch.

13

I opened my eyes.

There was a bright light above me, which made my head wreck with agony right away. The buzzing, static sound that I'd heard back on the island was still there, grating in my mind. I could taste blood, and my muscles felt weak and heavy.

But I was still alive. That had to count for something.

I was still here.

I lifted my head and looked around. I was in some kind of cell. Outside the cell, I could hear chatter and footsteps. I could see other cells just like this, towering up above. I had no idea where I was exactly, but I could have a good guess: Saint's very own tower.

Saint built this tower very soon after his assault on the planet. It didn't take much to erect it. He already had the plans in place, and he more than had the abilities to put it all together. Besides, he had ULTRAbots working for him too, some of which I could see hovering around the tower right now.

I reached out to put my hands on the bars.

When I got within an inch, I felt a strong force build up under my palms then throw me back across the room.

I slammed against the back wall. The dim light shuddered. I brushed myself down, heart pounding, and went to stand again.

That's when I saw I wasn't alone in this cell.

Stone was standing over me. To my left, Ember, Vortex, Roadrunner, Orion. The last remnants of the original Resistance, all of us trapped in here.

Stone didn't look too happy to see me.

"What hap—"

"You little asshole!"

Stone wrapped his hands around my throat. His arms and fingers solidified into rock right away. I could see him struggling as that electricity repressing our powers intensified. But he kept on gripping anyway, trying to squeeze the life from me.

I struggled. Tried to hit back. I couldn't get him free of me. My powers were too dampened.

"You tried to kill me," Stone said. "Held me under the damned water and tried to drown me."

"I—I—"

"You knew damned well I'd come outta my trance. You knew damned well that douchebag had stopped controlling me. But you kept on going, didn't you? You just had to keep on going."

I tried to break free. I looked at Orion, Ember, Roadrunner, and Vortex, waited for some kind of help from them. But they just let Stone keep on gripping my neck. Allowed him to squeeze the life out of me.

"I was just—"

"Time for excuses is up, Kyle. Time for excuses died when you held me under that water."

"Please. I just thought—"

"How's it feel, hmm? Seeing the light yet?"

I could see a light above me. But there was a weird sensation too. I felt like I'd been in a position like this before, held down, unable to breathe.

And it felt like Orion had stood beside me that time, too.

As my consciousness slipped further, the voices and noises around me fading into the background, I felt that blurry memory becoming clearer.

The water.

The presence beside me.

The voices...

I felt myself sinking further into the warmth of that memory, praying for it to take over me completely.

Then Stone loosened his grip and stepped aside. "You watch yourself, kid. Next time, you won't be so lucky."

I rubbed at my neck. Stone's hands had bruised it, bad. I looked up and saw the rest of the crew scowling at me. Orion just stood there observing.

"So what's the plan?" I gasped, eager to move on to the more urgent matter of getting out of this place.

Orion paced around the cell. "The anti-energy currents running through this room are strong."

"Not strong enough to hold the six of us, surely."

"Stronger than any I have ever encountered."

I didn't want to accept that, but I could *feel* the anti-energy squeezing my powers as I walked around the cell. It felt like my head might burst. "The island. Is it—"

"Taken? Yes."

My stomach knotted. "And the rest of the Resistance?"

Orion lowered his head.

"Lot of 'em dead," Ember said. "Some of 'em still living. Most of 'em, we don't have a clue where they are."

"They split us up," Stone said. "And *you* didn't help matters."

"Look," I said. "I saw someone was controlling you all. I tried to stop him."

"You tried to kill me."

"Yes. Yes, I did. But only because—"

"'Only because' what? Because you thought it might get you closer to Saint? 'Cause you thought as long as you put Saint through a little bit of pain, nobody else mattered?"

I didn't want to answer that question. Of course I wanted revenge for everything Saint had done. But at the expense of my people—my ULTRAs, my Resistance? That was way off the mark.

"Look," I said. "I know... I know what I did was wrong. And I'm sorry for that. Really."

Stone didn't look too convinced.

"But right now, our focus should be on getting out of this place."

"I already told you," Orion said. "It's too strong."

I smiled. Shook my head. "You really think I'm gonna take that for an answer?"

Orion looked at me, as did the others. Vortex had a smile on her face now too.

"These bars and these walls might be tough. But we're gonna break out of them and we're gonna get out of this place."

"And then what?" Roadrunner asked.

"Hmm?"

"When we get out of here? Then what?"

I knew what she was getting at. The whole world had fallen. We had nowhere to go to. All we could do? Fight.

"We'll figure that out when we figure *this* out," I said. "You ready?"

There was a moment where the faces of my peers looked happy. Optimistic. But that soon diminished.

They were looking outside the cell bars.

I felt someone's presence there. A presence I knew I'd felt before already.

I held my breath. Turned around. I couldn't accept my suspicions. I couldn't believe they could possibly be true.

When I saw who was standing there, all of my optimism crumbled.

"Hello, Kyle," Daniel Septer—Nycto—said. "We're making an awful bad habit of bumping into one another lately, aren't we?"

14

"Well? Aren't you even going to say hello to your old friend?"

I walked along the metal walkway, Nycto moving behind me. My hands were tied behind my back with some kind of cuffs that repressed my power, like a more focused form of the energy in the cells. Nycto had got me out of the cell and left the rest of my peers in there. I had no idea where he was taking me, only that wherever it was couldn't be good.

I looked around at the tower. It was even bigger than I'd first thought. The cell openings stretched on further than I could see. Above, I saw little hovering specks. I didn't know what they were at first until it clicked that they were ULTRAbots.

"Quite something this place, isn't it?"

I felt a knot in my throat every time I heard Nycto speak. "I thought you were supposed to be dead?"

"Well, I probably should be. I mean, you should've killed me when you had the chance. But you didn't, *things* happened, and then here we are."

"Saint. He knocked you out of the sky like an annoying little fly."

"He did. And it hurt; I'm not going to lie. It took me some time to regain my pride and confidence after that. But when I did, I saw the way the world was. I saw just how glorious and powerful Saint was, and how much I could help him."

"You sound just as insane as ever."

Nycto chuckled. I felt him tighten his mind powers around my throat. "I always love it when you say that."

We walked further down the metal walkway. We must've been walking a while because my knees were starting to ache.

"I didn't just back down," Nycto said, continuing his droning on. "I rediscovered my strength. I fought my way in here and told Saint how things were. What I could offer him."

"A running commentary?"

Again, Nycto laughed. "If there's one thing I like about you, it's your sense of humor."

"I wish I could find one thing I liked about you. Just to even it out."

"Well, we always seem to keep crossing paths. That has to count for something, right?"

I didn't know whether to laugh or cry.

I looked at the cells as I passed. Unlike the one I'd been kept in, they were all faded out. I couldn't see through them. "More ULTRAs in here than I expected."

Another laugh from Nycto.

"That wasn't a joke. That wasn't even *meant* to be a joke."

"You'll see the comedy of your words soon."

He pressed my shoulders down. Up ahead, I saw a dip in the passageway. So we were going down. Far, far down.

We walked further. Passed more of these cells. On the way, we passed ULTRAbots too. They all seemed to glare at me but didn't even acknowledge Nycto's presence.

"Oh, we programmed them to accept us," Nycto said. "But

you... well, they still see you as a target. It's just a good job I'm with you, or I hate to see what'd happen."

"If you're so hell-bent on destruction, then why don't you just kill me?"

Nycto took a few seconds to respond. "I think I'd miss your comedy."

The further we descended, the more anxious I got about where we were going. It seemed to be getting more chaotic the further down we got. To my left, I saw some ULTRAbots zapping inside a cell, heard a few whimpers. There was a smell of metal in the air. Hot metal. All of it melded together to create a pretty unpleasant atmosphere.

"It's a pity you couldn't see the light like I did."

"Serving Saint's the light? Serving the person who killed my sister? Who killed my mom?"

"He killed my father, too. Made my upbringing a misery. But I look back on those sixteen miserable years now and I'm thankful for what he did. Because he made the anger build up inside me. And although the powers must've been dormant in me for years, it was only through the anger that they finally surfaced."

"I think I preferred you when you were a scrawny little nerd."

"Ah, yes. Being scrawny little nerds. Another thing we had in common before."

"Wow. Touché."

I saw a door right in front of us then. There was no left and no right, just this door. I knew there was only one outcome: we were heading toward it.

"Daniel, it's not too late to turn around."

Nycto laughed. "You always call me 'Daniel' when you're trying to appeal to a better nature you think I have."

"You must have some sense in your skull. I mean, you've

seen what Saint wants, really. He doesn't want us ULTRAs now he's got the ULTRAbots. And if he's told you you're special, then there must be something in it for him."

Nycto brought me to a stop, right outside the door. His grip around my already aching neck was tighter than ever. "He told me I'm special because I *am* special, 'Glacies'. As for the ULTRAs being worthless to him, perhaps at first. But not anymore. Not anymore at all."

He lifted a hand and opened up that door.

What I saw inside wasn't exactly what I expected.

The room was massive. It was spacious and airy. And it was filled with beds. Metal beds stretching out further in each direction than the eye could see.

And on those beds, there were people.

"If they're ULTRAs then that's how you're going to turn out too," I said. "You'll end up unconscious on a slab, just like them."

Again, Nycto laughed. He patted my shoulder, with his hand or his telekinesis, I wasn't sure. "Kyle, Kyle. These aren't ULTRAs at all. These are humans."

I felt my knees go weak. "What?"

"These beds are filled with humans. And when they are emptied, they will be filled with more humans. And more. And more, until eventually, there's no humans left."

My chest tightened. My heart pounded. I felt a shiver go up my spine when I looked at the still, sleeping bodies of all these people. "What... what do you want with the humans?"

Nycto stepped in front of me. For the first time since we'd started descending, he looked me right in the eyes with a smile. "We turn every single one of them into mindless slaves to do our bidding. Every single one."

[15]

"Kyle? Are you okay?"

I heard Vortex's words, but I didn't *hear* them, not really. My mind and attention were too focused on what I'd seen behind that door; what Nycto had shown me.

The rows and rows of humans, all stacked up, all ready to be brainwashed.

And the most selfish thing of all? When I saw those humans, it wasn't just any old face I saw on them. It was Damon's. Ellicia's. Dad's.

All people I loved, about to be taken away and turned into something else entirely.

Vortex touched my arm. I flinched.

"You've barely said a word since you got back here looking like you've seen one of my visions or something."

"Trust me," I said. "This was worse."

Vortex didn't look too pleased that anything could be worse than one of the visions she created.

"I saw people," I said. "Lots of people. People from the world below all stacked up and ready to be turned."

"Turned into what?" Orion asked.

I didn't even want to say the words. "Into autonomous beings."

I told the group about what I'd seen down there. About what Nycto had told me. Saint's next stage of the plan was to use humans. To make the most of them, treating them like natural resources.

"It fits in with Saint's MO," Orion said. "He never wanted to destroy humanity. It's never been his goal. To him, control is a much more attractive option."

"I just don't get how he can do this," Ember said.

"Huh?"

"I don't get how he can just wipe the minds of people. I mean, that's gotta take some man and woman power, right?"

"Maybe so," Orion said. "But Saint created the ULTRA-bots. He managed to intercept the US government and turn it against itself. He's a very, very clever individual, to his credit. It's just a shame his heart is in the wrong place."

"Heart," Stone spat. "Bastard ain't got no heart."

I caught Orion glancing at me then. Weirdly, he still had that bowler hat and black mask of his on, which he wore at all times. It was as if it was welded to his face. There were rumors that it was part of a failed shielding experiment in the early days of his career, and that he was unable to remove it. But it did make me wonder.

"Did he show you what he was using to wipe their minds?" Ember asked.

I tried to remember what I'd seen down in that awful room. "No. He just... he said they had something. Or someone."

"Did he say who they were?" Orion interrupted.

I was surprised by how quick he snapped. He was usually so collected. It was weird to hear him breaking that now. "No. Why?"

He shook his head. "Nothing. I just..."

"Is there something you're not telling us?"

Orion looked around at the rest of the cell. He must've realized everyone was looking at him. "I don't know. All I know is that Saint is very powerful. More powerful than ever before. And with the mind-controller in his wake, I guess... perhaps he's found a way to channel his powers to wipe the human mind. I'm not sure. I'm really not sure."

The rest of the ULTRAs looked away from Orion. I kept looking at him. I wasn't convinced he was being completely honest.

"Whatever the case," I said, "we can't sit around in here because Saint doesn't have good plans for us."

"So what do you suggest we do?" Vortex asked.

I looked around the cell. I felt that energy, strong, fighting against me. "When I was in my cuffs, I tried to use my powers, but obviously the energy soaked them up and stopped them."

"Tell us something we don't know," Stone said.

"But there was a moment," I said. "A split second moment where I felt like I was free of them. If we could just somehow focus on that moment... really hone in on it, using our powers together, I think I can get us out of this place. But we'll need to all be in it. And we'll need to all be prepared."

"Prepared for what?" Stone asked.

I swallowed a lump in my throat. "For it not to go to plan."

I heard sighs around the cell. The uncertainty and frustration were paramount. And I could get it. I wanted to be anywhere but here right now. I wanted to be fighting Saint, taking him down, making him pay. But I knew right now my priority was getting out of here, and getting my fellow ULTRAs out of here. Then, we could fight back.

"Grab my hands," I said.

I felt Vortex's fingers slip into mine. Then I felt Orion take my other hand. We stood in a circle, the energy between us strong but not strong enough to fight the energy. Not right now.

But we could work up to it. We could fight.

"So what exactly we supposed to do?" Stone asked. "Stand around like some kind of wacky séance and hope for the best?"

"Just... just focus on that resistance in the air. Just focus on it. And when you feel that moment of total power, you throw all your anger and pain and love into it. We do that together."

"And how do we know we're all gonna feel it at the same time?" Roadrunner asked.

I had to be honest. "We don't. But we just have to try. Okay?"

Roadrunner sighed then nodded. "Let's go."

I focused on the things that angered me the most. I tried to bring love into it too, but all I saw was Saint. All I saw was his destruction. The pain and the chaos he'd caused.

And as I focused on that pain inside, I felt the magnetic resistance getting stronger. I felt my muscles tightening. My brain felt hot, like it was boiling.

"Not sure I can do this!" Stone shouted.

"Hold on!"

I gripped Vortex's and Orion's hands harder. I could feel that moment coming. The moment where we could embrace our powers. We were going to do this. We were going to get out of here. We were—

A crack.

A smash of light above.

The cell filled with darkness.

We all fell down and hit the ground. Vortex gasped, as did the others. Orion held his back, wincing.

"It's too tough," Ember said. "We'll never do it."

"We can if we try. We were close. We just have to give it another shot. We just have to—"

"Go on then. Give it another shot. But just see how far it gets you."

The Scottish accent sounded familiar—like I'd heard it before recently.

When I looked at the cell door where the voice came from, I knew exactly why.

Controlla was standing there.

And he was lifting his hands and getting ready to control.

16

I felt Controlla's powers wrap around me right away.

The cell around me disintegrated from my consciousness. I knew Orion, Ember, Roadrunner, Vortex and Stone were there, but they seemed far away. I could hear voices. Voices of those I loved crying out for me to help. I could see Ellicia somewhere in the distance, clouded in the fog. I wanted to get to her and help her, but I couldn't move a muscle.

"You know what the problem with trying to escape this place is?" Controlla asked. He walked toward me, his footsteps heavy. He seemed to be growing in height with every single step. His powers were similar to Vortex's, only much stronger, and much more persuasive. That was a terrifying thought.

I tried to speak back to Controlla but couldn't move my lips.

"Every time you try to use your powers, we get a signal. And every time we get a signal, we get excited. Because you know what it means when we get a signal?"

Controlla stood right opposite me now. His face was in flames. His grin was wide and beaming.

"It means we get to put you through hell."

I felt a searing pain in my chest and the whole cell around me vanished.

I was on the street. It was snowing. I knew what day it was because I could see the fight in the sky just above.

Just ahead, I saw Cassie running to me, fear in her eyes.

I wanted to tell her to turn around. To go over there and stop her. But I wasn't in control. Saint and Orion were too caught up in battle. There was no stopping them, and there was no stopping Cassie.

But I fought anyway. I fought and with all my strength, I managed to lift my heavy foot. I resisted the energy grip and lifted my other foot, and before I knew it, I was running.

It wracked my body with agony, but I powered nearer to Cassie. I wasn't watching her die again.

She looked at me and shouted something. I couldn't hear what anymore, her words were so drowned out by the chaos above, and by the crackling static sound in my skull.

"It's okay," I shouted, as I got within inches of her, closer than I'd ever got in any of my dreams. "I've got you."

I went to grab her hands.

Her hands disintegrated on contact.

I stood there, then, stunned. I watched as Cassie's body crumbled away before me, fell to dust.

"No."

And then, behind her, I saw Mom. She was crying, while her fingers also fell to dust.

"No!"

I felt the pain of my own scream echo all around. I knew this was a nightmare that Controlla was putting me through. I had no idea what I was doing with my physical body, and I figured that was how he worked. He manipulated the mind with nightmares like this and got people to do dirty deeds.

I could have my hands around Stone's neck.

I could be beating Ember.

I could be...

Another flash. This time, it was so vivid, so rich. It felt like I had control of this, though. Like it was a part of my consciousness, not Controlla's.

The underwater memory. Only it was much stronger than I'd ever had it.

There was someone else beside me, to the right.

And then there was someone else to the left, too.

I felt their fingertips touch mine, and in that instant, total power between us. Total bond.

I felt the figure above me lift me out the water.

I focused on that memory with everything I had. I could feel Controlla's grip weakening. But I just had to see what was in the memory. I had to know the truth. I had the feeling it was important. I'd always suspected it was one of my life's biggest secrets, and still I didn't totally get it.

A muffled voice I didn't recognize as the figure lifted me from the water.

As I turned and saw a boy beside me.

And then I heard another cry to my right, and I turned to look and—

A blast cracked through the memory.

I was back in the cell again. Controlla was lying on his back on the other side of the cell door.

The cell door was open.

All around me, my friends were still. They stared at me, wide-eyed.

"What the hell did you just do?" Stone asked.

I looked at my hands. I could still feel the fingertips from my memory. "I don't..."

I heard Controlla start to groan as he came back round.

I knew what I had to do.

"Get out of here."

I flew out of the cell. Landed on Controlla's chest. I lifted my fist and I punched him, right in his face.

He fought back. Tried to grip my neck. I felt him trying to worm his way into my mind, but every time he got close, I embraced all my anger and hit him again, and again.

After a while of hitting him, I didn't see Controlla underneath me at all. I saw Saint. I saw all the pain he'd caused, and I knew I couldn't just back away from this level of anger, not anymore.

"Kyle!"

I heard the muffled cry of my voice as I squeezed my telekinetic grip tighter around Controlla's neck.

"You don't have to do this!"

"Do it," Controlla spat. "Prove who you really are. *What* you really are."

I dug my teeth into my bottom lip.

Took in a deep breath of the clammy, metallic air.

And then I swung a power-charged fist down into Controlla's face.

Hard.

17

I slammed my fist into Controlla's face.

At least I intended to.

My fist stopped just centimeters from his nose. Something was stopping me hitting him.

It took me a few seconds to see that it was Orion using his powers to stop me.

"We need to go, Kyle," Orion said.

I tightened my fist and tried to push even harder. I was too in the zone to leave. I wanted to punish Saint for everything he'd done, and that meant punishing the people close to Saint. "I can't just go."

"Remember our rules," Orion said, sternly, keeping a steady focus on containing my powers. "We do not kill our own. No matter what."

I looked down into Controlla's eyes and for a split second, I saw the normal person underneath. He was just a kid like me. Someone who'd discovered he had abilities. He'd chosen to use them in a shitty way and for a bad cause, sure. But he was just another ULTRA.

"We'll come for you," Controlla said. "And everyone you care about. If there's anyone left alive."

My sympathy disappeared in an instant. I pushed through Orion's resistance and got closer to Controlla's face. My hand was covered in ice right now. Some of it was spraying out, bouncing off a shield Orion was doing all he could to keep in place.

"Kyle, stop this. Remember who you are."

"Do it," Controlla said. "And see who you *really* are."

"I want to," I gasped. I kept on pressing downwards. "You've no idea how much I want to."

"Then show me."

Controlla smiled.

He lifted his head closer to the blast of ice powering toward his forehead.

Then I heard blasts to my left.

I looked across. There were six ULTRAbots hovering in the air.

And they were firing at the Resistance and me.

"Come on, Kyle!"

I looked down at Controlla as the ULTRAbots closed in. All around, an alarm sounded, so loud that it covered the sounds of the ULTRAbots' blasts.

"Finish me while you've got the chance."

To my right, I saw Orion, Roadrunner, Ember, Stone and Vortex running away from the cell.

"I've not finished with you yet," I said.

I fired two blasts of ice around Controlla's wrists, tying him to the floor.

Then I stood up and ran after the Resistance.

The blasts of the ULTRAbots' guns fired all around us. More of them swarmed up from the massive opening in the middle of the tower. And above, I saw them descending closer to us.

"Did anyone think to check where the exit is in this place?" Stone shouted.

I looked all around. We were on a level we couldn't get off. "Grab my hand."

"Oh, not this again," Stone said.

"Just do it."

We all linked hands as the ULTRAbots approached. I held my breath. Closed my eyes. Focused everything on teleporting out of here.

A crushing pain cracked through my head.

I fell down, and so too did the rest of the Resistance.

"Well that worked a treat!" Stone shouted.

"There must be some kind of block on the walls of this place stopping us leaving," Vortex said.

"So what the hell are we supposed to do?"

I looked back at the oncoming ULTRAbots. "I have an idea."

"What? Stand there gawping at the things that're gonna kill us?"

"Vortex. You can control the ULTRAbots, right?"

She shook her head. "I... I can get into the head of *an* ULTRAbot—"

"Then you get in its head and you work on controlling it."

"I can't control anything, Kyle. It's not my power."

"If Controlla can do it then so can you."

"That's not necessarily true," Orion said.

"So what the hell else are we supposed to do?"

We all stood our ground and looked at the crowd of ULTRAbots facing us.

"We fight," Orion said.

I watched the ULTRAs around me jump up into the blasts

of the ULTRAbots' guns. Ember shot flames at three of them, disintegrating them on impact. Vortex had two of them gripping their helmets, crashing into one another in the confusion. Stone was hopping from one to the other, smashing heads left right and center, Roadrunner helping dizzy them in confusion.

Orion was drifting around, dodging their bullets, moving just as smoothly as I knew he could all this time.

I stood there and looked up at this fight. I looked up above at the tower. I could go up there. I could take down Saint. I could end all this, right here, right now.

Then I saw a massive blast from an ULTRAbot gun hurtling toward me.

I was too late to dodge it. It hit me in the chest. I flew back and crashed into the wall of the tower. When I hit, I felt a little singe of pain as the anti-energy force bit me. But there was something else, too. The ULTRAbots' ammo. It had made a little hole in the wall.

I hovered there then. Waved my arms to get the ULTRAbots' attention. There was an absolute swarm of them now.

"Hey!" I shouted, my chest still painful. "Over here!"

The ULTRAbots all hovered up and surrounded me.

Lifted their guns.

Fired.

I dodged their bullets, one by one. I felt the pain of the wall's resistance against me. But I could feel the wall weakening. I could sense our way out opening up.

I saw a huge bullet of energy right in front of my face.

I ducked down. For a moment, I was convinced that was it. I'd had it.

Then there was a massive, electronic blast right behind me.

I felt fresh air. I looked around and saw there was an opening. The wall was crumbling away.

"Get out of here!" I cried.

I watched Ember battle his way to the opening and fired ice at the ULTRAbots as Vortex, Roadrunner, and Orion fought their way out, too.

"Stone, quick!"

The ULTRAbots were all around Stone. All surrounding him. I tried to fire at them, take them down, but more and more of them just kept on spawning around him.

"We've gotta go," Ember said.

I watched as the ULTRAbots closed in on Stone. As he punched them back as hard as he could.

"Kyle," Orion said. "We've got to go."

The ULTRAbots surrounded Stone.

His punches got weaker.

Then, he stopped punching them away altogether.

[18]

Saint never liked being disappointed.

He looked at the cells where the captured Resistance had been kept. They were supposed to be so secure, yet here they were, completely empty. In the distance, he saw a gaping hole in the wall of his tower. He could feel a breeze brushing through it and it made him feel sick.

"How on earth did something like this happen?"

He tried to keep his cool as he turned to look at Controlla. He'd never been one for losing his temper, especially not with his own. Losing his temper just lowered the morale of everybody working for him. He couldn't have morale lowering. Not when they were so close to such a beautiful moment.

Controlla glared at the floor. He rubbed the back of his head. He was just a boy. Naive to the demands of the world he lived in. "Something... something just happened."

"You're supposed to get inside the minds of others, aren't you?"

Controlla nodded. "I did. I got inside Kyle's mind—"

"Then what happened?"

"I... I don't know. Something I've never seen before. Like he reversed it. Bounced it back at me. Then it was too late."

Saint gritted his teeth. He resisted the urge to lash out, as much as his powers tingled at his fingers.

He took a deep breath and walked further across the metal flooring.

On the ground up ahead, there were pieces of rubble. Small chunks of debris. "But you managed to stop one of them leaving, by the looks of things. Right?"

Again, Controlla lowered his head, breaking Saint's gaze.

"The one who calls himself Stone. You stopped him. Right?"

"The—the ULTRAbots had him. Then something happened there too. He got away before they could finish him. But I swear I tried to help stop him. I swear I did everything I could."

Saint scanned Controlla's face. He didn't really like him. He was one of the ULTRAs Nycto had brought along with him, insisting he could be an asset. Saint gave him the benefit of the doubt. Already he was starting to regret his generosity.

"What happened," Controlla said, as the ULTRAbots worked on putting the tower wall back together. "If I could've stopped it, I would. But I gave it my everything. I swear."

Saint put a hand on Controlla's shoulder. Smiled. "Come with me. There's something I'd like to show you."

He led Controlla down the steps. Right down, toward the room where he kept the humans. The first batch of humans, almost ready for their big moment. The first test of just how powerful he actually was—of just how powerful *they* actually were.

He opened the door and held a hand out for Controlla to go first. They stepped into the room and looked around.

"I always find it so peaceful down here," Saint said, his voice echoing. "So soothing, being here with all these sleeping souls."

He walked up to the first human. A woman with dark brown hair and soft skin. He put a hand on her stomach.

"But it excites me, too. Because I realize now just how amazing it'll be when they finally wake from their sleep in service of us. Come over here."

Controlla looked hesitant. His eyes were wide.

Saint waved him over. "Please. Join me. I'd like you to see what we can do."

After a few seconds of hesitation, Controlla walked over to Saint's side. They stood together at the foot of the bed where the woman lay. Saint put his hands on the bottom of the bed, and Controlla joined him on the other side. Together, they pushed the woman through a door right ahead, into a darkened room.

It smelled so damp in this room. It really could do with redecorating. But it would be fine, for now. He hadn't exactly built it with first-class accommodation in mind.

"Where are we going?"

Saint walked a little further. Then he stopped right in front of a blacked out window. "We're right here."

There was silence for a moment.

Then Saint whistled.

Behind the blacked out window, a blue light grew. It completely lit up the room, shone through the window, and its beam hovered over the body of the woman.

Controlla looked on in awe as the light beamed down onto the woman's chest. Her body twitched. Her fingers shook. Something was happening.

"Imagine this process but magnified," Saint said. "Imagine what we could do if we had more power like this. That is the goal. That is the endgame."

The blue light intensified. For a moment, Saint looked into

the eyes of the girl behind the glass. The girl who had these marvelous abilities.

And then the light disappeared and it was dark again.

Saint lifted his hand. Lit up the air.

The woman on the bed was still.

"What's... what's supposed to have happened?" Controlla asked.

He didn't have to wait long for his answer.

The woman's eyes opened.

She shot up and wrapped her hands around his neck.

He shook as he fought against her on the ground. Saint knew he was trying to use his powers, but he made sure they were repressed as the human woman—now under his total control—held him to the ground.

"This is the difference between your kind and my kind," Saint said, as Controlla shouted out, screamed. "This is the difference between the first wave of ULTRAs, and ULTRAbots and humans totally under my control."

"Please!" Controlla shouted, writhing on the floor. "Don't do this!"

Saint smiled. He took a deep breath of the damp air and looked through the blackened glass. He knew she was in there somewhere. "Oh, it's done, my child. It's done. And this is just the beginning."

Controlla cried out again.

Then, he went silent.

I blasted through the sky and away from the ULTRAbots.

It was dark. I wasn't sure where we were exactly, just that we'd escaped Saint's tower a while back. We'd had to shake off several ULTRAbots on our way, but we'd dealt with them. Of course we had. We were much stronger than them.

The rain lashed down. The waves beneath us were strong and tall. It was pitch black other than the unnatural light we created between us. There was me, Orion, Vortex, Stone, Roadrunner and Ember. We'd made our way out of Saint's tower.

Well. Stone had almost fallen.

"Why's it always me who gets the heroic near-death moments?" Stone shouted.

Vortex giggled. "Better that way than the *actual* death moments."

Stone scratched at a missing chunk of rock on his arm. "Damn. Not so sure about that anymore."

I heard the rest of the Resistance bickering, but I wasn't really listening. I just stared back in the direction we'd come from, into the storm.

"So where to now we've got no home?" Ember asked.

"There's bound to be some other uninhabited islands," Vortex said. "Or we could just use Stone as an island."

"I heard that."

"I hoped you would."

"Kyle?"

I looked to my right. Orion, Roadrunner, and Ember were hovering there beside me. Each of them looked concerned.

"What's going on in your head, man?" Ember asked.

I looked back into the storm. "I just... Saint. He's right there in his tower."

Orion sighed. "We've discussed this."

"We've proven we can fight what he throws at us."

"We don't know for sure he's thrown everything at us," Orion said.

"But just knowing he's still in there, in that tower. We were so close. I was... I was so close. And I just ran away."

"You *flew* away because if you hadn't, you'd have died in there."

"I wouldn't have died."

"We're fighting a war," Orion said. "And no wars were ever won by rash, haphazard decisions. We don't go flying into a tower without knowing what we're getting into. You saw what they had planned yourself with those humans. Who knows what other secrets they've got waiting inside?"

I looked down at the sea. I knew Orion had a point. "I just... I just can't keep on running while the ULTRA responsible for my family's death is still in there ruling—"

"Kid, he didn't just kill your damned family," Stone shouted.

"I meant... I meant *our* families."

"No you didn't," Orion said.

His words surprised me. "Of course I did."

"You didn't, Kyle. And that's where the problem lies. I don't believe you are fighting this battle for us. I don't believe you're fighting this battle for anyone but yourself."

"That's rubbish."

"Every decision you make, you make it in your own self-interest. You go rushing after Saint in the Battle for Manchester. You hold Stone under the water just because you think he's possessed by someone close to Saint."

"I've told you, I didn't mean that."

"And you're going to rush into near-certain death, all because you're so hell-bent and vengeful. Well, I'm sorry, Kyle, but we aren't going to be by your side to do that. Not without a plan."

I watched as Orion drifted away from me and I couldn't believe what I was seeing.

"Stone? Roadrunner? Ember? Vortex? Surely you aren't gonna just give up too?"

There was sadness in Vortex's eyes. "I'm sorry," she said, drifting away with Orion. "But I'm with Orion. We can't risk everything when we have no idea how to truly weaken the enemy we're facing."

"Ember? Roadrunner? You're in this with me too, right?"

Ember shook his head and drifted back, so too did Roadrunner. "I'm sorry, man. There's just been too much loss as it is. Can't risk anyone else."

I looked at Stone, totally defeated. I knew he wouldn't be with me right away. "What happened," I said. "Back at the waterfall. It was wrong. But I only did it because—"

"Come back to us when you actually give a damn about us, kid," Stone said. "Get the hell over yourself. There's a war to fight."

He floated backward, joining Vortex, Ember, Roadrunner, and Orion.

I stared up at them, a knot in my stomach. I felt the divide between us. They thought I'd caused this rift, all because I was trying to take down Saint. "We need to be together. To fight this war. We can't win alone."

"And that's what *you* need to remember," Orion said. "Not us. *You* need to remember that."

He hesitated. Stopped drifting away. For a moment, I was convinced he was going to stop and fly back down here, tell me he had my back. Or at least forgive me for whatever he thought I'd done wrong.

But then a flash of lightning filled the sky. Made me blink.

When I opened my eyes, Orion and the Resistance were gone.

I was all alone with the crashing waves and the rapid wind, the storm clouds getting thicker overhead.

[20]

I looked down at the island where everyone I cared about lived and I knew I should be far, far away from here.

It was night. It was always night when I came here. Even though I could turn invisible at the click of a finger, I still didn't want to risk being spotted in the light of day. Or maybe I was worried about me seeing someone else. Maybe I was worried about what'd happen if I saw my dad walking around in the daylight, or Damon laughing and joking with Avi, or Ellicia's beautiful face.

There was a lump in my throat as I looked down from the top of the tree at the village. It was calm, and most people were inside. On the silence of this island, it was hard to believe that the rest of the world had fallen. I knew nowhere was safe, especially not now Saint had some unsavory plans for humans. But I'd fight. I'd fight like hell to keep this place safe.

I hoped it wouldn't have to come to that, though.

There was another reason I was here too. After the rest of the Resistance had left me behind following the escape of Saint's tower, I'd thought about going back there. Fighting Saint myself. I was tough, and I could take on whatever he could throw at me.

But I knew if I did that, I'd probably fail. And if I failed, I was worried about what it might mean for the people I loved.

I looked down at the little building where Ellicia was living. I wanted to go in there and speak with her. I needed to tell her I was going to stop Saint. But I didn't want to put her in any danger, and it felt like just by revealing myself to the people of this island, I'd be putting them in danger.

And there was Dad, too. I needed to speak to him. Dad used to be full of wisdom, even when he'd slipped into his depression. He'd been the one to talk me through my exams at school; given me loads of little mental tips and pieces of advice that'd got me through all kinds of dramas in my life.

I needed to know what to do. I needed to know how to go about all this.

I needed him to tell me to get revenge against Saint.

But something made me worry he wouldn't tell me that at all.

Orion seemed insistent about his "no kill" thing. It was limiting us in the war. Sure, it was all fair and well in an ideal-istic world where all ULTRAs could peacefully co-exist, but the truth was, the likes of Nycto and Saint didn't want peace. There was no room for them in this world. As long as they existed, the world was under threat.

Only by destroying them both could we ever dream of a normal world again.

Well. Not normal. The world would never be normal after all that'd happened.

But at least it could breathe again.

I hopped off the tree, steadied my fall with my powers, and walked over to the door of Dad's house. I was just going to go in there and ask him, straight up, what he thought I should do.

How I should go about this battle. I had to keep as much emotion out of it as possible. I had to be professional. I couldn't stick around—I had to stay as detached as I could.

I stepped up to the door. Held my breath. My pulse raced in my throat.

And then I stepped right through the walls.

I saw Dad right away. He was lying on a little bed barely a foot off the ground. By his side, there was a small flashlight. He was holding something in his hands.

As I got closer, still invisible, I realized Dad was holding a photograph of me, him and Mom. It'd been taken just a few months before Mom's death. One of the happier post-Glacies days. We'd started spending more time together, and we went on a trip up to Niagara Falls. We'd got soaked and had a blast. I'd even sneakily saved a kid from slipping into the water and stopped a boat from capsizing, all without anyone even noticing. But the highlight of the day was just sitting in a diner afterward, exhausted from the long day, and watching the sunset with Mom and Dad by my side. All of us smiling, joking, not talking about past memories, but creating new ones.

It was perfect.

I noticed then that Dad was crying.

I walked closer to him. Crouched down beside him. He still hadn't noticed me, so strong was my invisibility.

He peered at the photograph, which shook in his hand. Tears streamed down his cheeks. His jaw shook.

"I miss you," he whispered. "I miss you both so much."

I felt a lump in my throat. My eyes started to sting. Poor Dad had lost everybody. He'd had everyone taken away from him. Usually when I thought about this, it made me feel angry. All the more determined to make Saint pay.

But right now, I just felt sadness.

I reached my hand out. Felt the warmth of Dad's arm

getting closer. I wanted to put a hand on it and reassure him. I wanted to hug him and tell him I was here for him, and that I wasn't ever going away again.

I got within an inch of his arm when I heard a scream outside.

Dad lunged out of the bed. I fell back, almost losing my invisibility, as he raced toward the door.

I looked around as he opened the door. Outside, more screams.

A humming noise.

And a light in the sky.

"What is it?" Dad shouted.

I already knew what it was, but I didn't want to admit it. I didn't want to accept it.

"It's the ULTRAbots," someone shouted. "They're here!"

I saw the ULTRAbots gathering around the island where everyone I loved lived and I knew what I had to do.

I shot out of my dad's house into the sky. I flew right at the ULTRAbots. There were so many of them. Hundreds. I knew what this was, as they hovered there in the sky, the island filled with the sounds of screams and the humming noises of the ULTRAbots. They were here to take this island. They were here to take my family. My friends.

I couldn't let them do that.

I watched as the ULTRAbots lifted their weapons. I knew how this would go. They'd fire a few stray shots to scare the island into submission. They'd deal with any troublemakers. Then the island would be theirs. I'd seen it happen so many times already. I knew the drill. Some of the humans would remain here, imprisoned. Some of them would go up to Saint's tower for a very different fate.

Now I knew what that fate was, I couldn't let it happen to the people I loved.

I flew into the middle of the ULTRAbots, still invisible. I

saw a few of them diverting their gaze from the island below, looking all around as I hopped between them, confusing them.

Then, when I knew my moment was right, I revealed myself, great spheres of ice in my hands.

"Everyone get inside!" I shouted.

I slammed my fists together and caused an explosion of ice. Tons of the ULTRAbots fell back. I heard their bullets fire at me and immediately forged a strong icy shield around myself. I bounced bullets back at the ULTRAbots. Threw them into one another. All of them were paying me attention now. None of them were focusing on the island anymore.

That's what I wanted.

I teleported upwards, away from the island, and recharged the ice in my hands. "Come on then!"

They all looked up at me.

Then they all lowered their guns.

Shot up toward me.

I was thrown by their speed and the fluidity of their movement. I felt their bodies slam into mine, knocking the wind out of me, hurting my ribcage. They must be newer models. Faster models. I knew Saint was always working to improve his ULTRAbot program, so I had to be prepared for whatever he threw at me.

I regained my composure and kicked the nearest ULTRAbot down. I punched the next one away, blasting it right across the sea.

Then I felt something grab my arm and press a gun to my chest.

I squeezed my eyes shut as the blast echoed through my skull.

Then I teleported behind the ULTRAbot before it could fire at me.

I fired ice into its back and sent it flying into oblivion.

I saw what I had to do then. There was a sphere of ULTRAbots all around me. I had to use my powers to teleport all of us away from here. This fight couldn't go on above the island. I could do with the aid of the Resistance. This wouldn't be easy.

I fired two blasts of ice up into the sky to distract the ULTRAbots.

Then, as time slowed down, as I focused down to the nearest millisecond, I poured all my anger into creating a sphere around us. An invisible sphere, starting in my hands, then widening. I felt it getting bigger. Felt its energy spreading. I could get us away from here. I could—

"Help!"

I heard a shout down below and I lost my grip of the sphere.

When I looked down, I saw Ellicia's dad, Mike. He was on the sand, lying on his back.

An ULTRAbot was above him, gun to his chest.

I wanted to get out of here, but the thought of Ellicia losing anyone pained me too much.

So I threw myself back down to the island.

I slammed into the ULTRAbot's back before it could fire at Mike, and I held it down on the sand.

I saw something, then. Something that made my skin go cold. This ULTRAbot. I recognized it. In fact, I'd seen it very recently.

And then it dawned on me in a sickening turn.

It wasn't an ULTRAbot at all.

It was a human.

One of the humans Saint had brainwashed. One of the ones I'd seen lying on those beds.

The woman beneath me punched me, hard, her powers way stronger than a human's. I went flying back into the air. I didn't want to hurt her. She was just a human, after all. ULTRAbots were robotic, so I didn't feel much sympathy when I took them down.

But humans... brainwashed humans. That was just wrong.

Still, I had to stop her.

I stretched out my hands, but then I felt something grab my shoulders, drag me up into the air. All around me, ULTRAbots and... well, I didn't want to think how many of those converted humans there were. I had to fight; I knew that much.

I pushed off a few of the ULTRAbots. I felt more cautious about blasting them with ice. I didn't want to be responsible for any death.

But Ellicia. Dad. My friends. They were down on that island. They needed protecting.

I looked back up at the circle of enemies above. I could still get them out of here, get them far away and put them somewhere they couldn't escape from. It's the only option I had.

I lifted my hand and focused my energy.

One by one, instead of ice, I fired those wormholes right into the chests of my enemies. I saw them vanish into thin air. Some of them exploded before they could vanish, and I knew for certain they were the ULTRAbots.

I kept on shooting them away, one by one. I knew it wouldn't be a permanent measure, but it'd buy me some time to save this island and make sure the people here got somewhere safe.

I was about to fire another blast when I heard an explosion underneath.

When I turned around, I saw all the houses in flames.

I felt a sickening blow cover me. A flashback to the fire at my house, which had taken Mom's life. I had to go down there and I had to help. I couldn't lose anyone else.

But then I saw the ULTRAbots and the humans move in

front of the burning village, blocking me from getting through them.

They all stood there, shielding the burning buildings. I heard screams below. Screams for help. And I felt totally and utterly defeated.

It was only then that I became aware of a presence behind me.

I looked back.

My fists tightened, and anger took over completely.

Nycto was hovering over the island.

His hands were filled with flames.

When I saw Nycto flying above the island, flames in his hands, I felt the urge for revenge tighten its grip once more.

I flew up toward him, into the dark sky. I could smell the smoke below and hear the cries of the people. But I had to make Nycto pay. He'd fought me, all this time. He'd caused so much hell, and he'd keep on causing hell if I didn't stop him.

If he'd hurt anyone else I cared about, I'd make him pay.

If he hadn't... well, I'd make him pay anyway.

I saw him just meters away. The flames in his hands were larger. He wasn't wearing his mask, and he was smiling.

"Catch," he said.

He threw the flames right at me.

Instinctively, I dodged them. But then I realized they were flying down to the island village, rapidly increasing in speed.

I flew back at them and fired them with ice.

The ice missed and hit a building down in the village.

It was then that I got an idea.

I fired a thick wall of ice right above the village and kept on going when I didn't think I could fire anymore. Kept on creating that gap between the village and the oncoming flames.

Nycto's fireballs blasted against the ice.

The ice soaked up the fire. It started to melt.

Then, in an instant, as the heat spread, it all turned into water and rained down on the burning village.

The flames diminished. The smoke got thicker, but at least it would give people down there more of a chance to get away. I'd be back to help them. I just had something else to do first.

When I turned, I saw that Nycto was gone.

For a moment, I felt total anger and frustration. I squeezed my hands together and let out a cry. I needed to stop him. He wasn't getting away. He wasn't causing any more pain.

Just as the anger totally controlled me, I saw a flash. It was of Nycto disappearing through a wormhole. He appeared some-where... somewhere light. The desert.

I saw these images like they were things I'd witnessed with my own eyes, then I flashed back to reality.

I knew my powers were strengthening. I could feel myself doing things I hadn't been capable of before.

Maybe that was an advantage to my desire for revenge that Orion just didn't accept.

I went through a wormhole of my own and focused on where I'd seen Nycto in that vision. A desert. Africa? Yes. It must've been. I'd seen animals like elephants in the background. I'd seen Kilimanjaro looming above.

I blasted myself to the exact spot I'd thought I saw Nycto.

When I got there, Nycto was already waiting.

He punched me right across the face. I fell back, smacking my head on the ground.

"You're like an annoying flea," he said. "You just never know when to stop biting, do you?"

I spat out some blood and stood. "I'll never stop. Not until I've made you pay."

"And the rest of your people. The rest of your freaks. Where are they now you need them most?"

"I don't need them. Not to take on a weak little shit like you."

Nycto grinned. Laughed. "Weak. Yeah. We'll see about that."

He lifted his hands, his fingers curled. I felt the ground beneath start to shake. Dust kicked up. In the distance, elephants and wildebeest ran away, terrified of whatever was coming.

"You put me at the bottom of a mountain and you showed me mercy," Nycto said, as the earth below started to crack. "I'll put you at the bottom of one. But I won't show you the same mercy."

It was then that I saw something in the corner of my eye, right behind Nycto.

Kilimanjaro was lifting into the air. The entire mountain was hovering above the ground.

It shifted in my direction as Nycto moved his hands.

I went to fire ice at Nycto to stop him. But then I saw all the animals under its shadow. I couldn't just make him drop Kilimanjaro. It'd cause so much death, so much destruction.

So I did the only thing I knew.

"You're not the only one with no more mercy, 'Daniel.'"

I lifted my hands and focused on Nycto. I felt my arms shake as I poured out energy into him. I wanted to teleport us both away from here. Not just us both, but Kilimanjaro too.

Wow. I was actually doing this. I was actually moving a goddamned mountain.

Kilimanjaro drifted further overhead. I felt its shadow cover me as I held my ground and tensed as hard as I could.

"You aren't stronger than me," Nycto gasped.

"Let's let actions speak louder than words."

"They are doing right now. And they're showing you aren't stronger than me."

"Just... just bear with me, at least. Give me a chance to find my footing. Jeez."

The more I pushed back, the more it felt like that shadow was surrounding me, blocking the sky above completely. I knew I was stronger than Daniel, but he was showing serious strength. Still, I had to keep on pushing. I couldn't just give up.

"Any last words, Kyle? Anything you want me to tell Ellicia and the other idiots who made the mistake of caring about you when we take them in? If they survive the fire, of course."

A sickening guilt washed over me. I was going to die. I was going to die and I wasn't going to be there to help the people I loved. "It's you who should think about the last words."

Nycto laughed. "Cute."

"You know what is cute?"

Nycto started lowering Kilimanjaro.

"Antarctica."

I blasted the pair of us—and Kilimanjaro—with as much power as I'd ever known over to Antartica.

When I landed on my back in Antartica, I saw Nycto hovering over me.

But above him, Kilimanjaro wasn't all solid anymore.

It'd broken up into small—well, still damn massive—but smaller meteor-like pieces.

"Hope you're better at dodgeball than you used to be," Nycto said.

He paused all the rocks in the sky. Re-directed them right over me.

And then he vanished.

The moment he did, the rocks started falling, flying down toward me like asteroids.

I guess that's the repayment I got for moving a mountain.

23

I held my breath as the remnants of Kilimanjaro fell down toward me.

Yes. I really was in a situation where one of the biggest mountains in the world had smashed to pieces and was heading in my direction. Lucky douchebag, right?

I raised my hands and fired a blast of ice at the massive rock nearest my face. I bolted to the right, sliding across the snow, and stopped three more huge pieces of rock slamming into the ground. It was like a game of Asteroid. I couldn't let this rock slam into Antartica or it might just split the continent in two, and who knew what that'd mean for the world.

I steered another of the large masses of land to a standstill. I heard more of the smaller rocks behind crash into it and couldn't see the sky for all the rocks above me.

I twisted my hands together, biting into my lip as the crumbling rocks all stuck together in the sky above. My arms shook. There were too many of them for me to hold. I wasn't sure what to do. One way or other, these rocks were going to collapse onto me. Nycto had gone. Back on the island where my family, friends, and girlfriend were, anything could be happening. I needed to get back to them and make sure they were safe.

The image of their homes igniting into flames filled me with fear.

I felt my arms getting weaker. I couldn't hold this rock much longer. The whole of Kilimanjaro hung above me. If I let go, even if I got out of the way, just the impact alone would cause chaos.

I lowered the fragments of Kilimanjaro down nearer to me, slowly. The closer it got, the heavier the weight grew. Soon, the first of the rocks were just meters from my face. Then inches. Then centimeters.

I felt a few little stones tumble against my face. I wasn't confident about what I was doing, but what other choice did I have?

I felt a lump swell in my throat and I pictured Ellicia, Dad, Damon, Avi.

"I'm coming for you."

Then I let my powers go and teleported above the debris.

I saw the rocks fall down and heard a massive bang crack across the landscape. I waited for the entire continent to split; for a shockwave to ripple across the planet.

It didn't.

As the snow fell, I looked down at the remains of Kiliman-jaro, out of place in the middle of the South Pole. I'd come close to losing that time. Too close.

Now I had to get back and make sure those I loved were safe.

I teleported back to the island. The sudden darkness was jarring and took me by surprise. Rain fell heavily. There was a humidity to the air.

Part of the reason for the humidity? The smoldering embers of the buildings below.

I floated down to the island. The air smelled of smoke. The buildings weren't burning as badly anymore, but there were still little flames. The foundations of the buildings had turned to ash.

There was no one around.

I lowered down to the ground, staying invisible even though I knew it wouldn't keep me hidden from the ULTRAbots. I snook past a few falling buildings. I had to check on Dad, Ellicia, Damon, and Avi. Of course it mattered that everyone on this island was safe, but they were my priority.

I got to Damon's place and my stomach sank.

There were flames crawling up the side of the building.

I wanted to go inside and see his fate for sure, but I knew what I'd see. I was too late. The battle with Nycto and then the wrangling with Kilimanjaro had taken too much time. I'd failed the people I cared most about.

Letting my guard drop, I floated over to Dad's house.

That too was in flames.

I couldn't bring myself to look inside, nor could I face checking Ellicia or Avi's houses. I knew exactly what I'd find. And yet the horror of the situation gnawed at me like a parasite. I was culpable in this. I'd had the choice to stay and fight for my family and friends, and girlfriend. Instead, I'd gone chasing after Nycto. Orion was right all along. Revenge was driving me to a place I didn't want to go.

I'd chosen to go after Nycto, and it'd got everyone I cared about killed.

I didn't know how to feel as I stood in the rain. My heart pounded. My invisibility had dropped completely. I didn't care whether someone came for me and took me away. All I cared about were the people I'd lost. The people I'd let down.

I went to walk away when I heard a noise above.

I activated my invisibility right away. There was a humming sound. The sound the ULTRAbots made.

But when I peered into the sky, I saw more than just ULTRAbots.

The ULTRAbots were lifting some of the island's people into the skies. Some of them were unconscious. Others were kicking and screaming.

They were taking them away, and I knew where to.

I took a step forward when I saw more ULTRAbots elevate. In their arms, more people. I knew that attacking them would only put the people at risk. As eager as I was to go and get my revenge and get these people back, I knew I needed a better plan.

When I saw the next group of people the ULTRAbots lifted into the air, that need for a plan grew all the more urgent.

First, Avi. He was kicking around, trying to fight free of their grip.

Then Damon. Ellicia. Dad.

All of them, eyes closed.

None of them aware of what was going on.

I tightened my fists and resisted the urge to fly up there and save them. They could've had their final thoughts before they were brainwashed and turned into Saint's slaves.

No. I wasn't going to let that happen.

I loosened my fists and watched them disappear into the sky as the rain lashed down all around me.

They were alive.

I was going to get them back.

I wasn't going to fail anyone else.

24

I t took four straight days of tracking Nycto's movements before I finally found him.

He was in the middle of the Amazon rainforest. He sat there alone, the birds singing around him. I wasn't sure what he was doing here, but I knew attacking him while he was in the tower was too dangerous. Orion was right—there were way too many defenses, and I'd only go and get myself killed. With everyone I cared about imprisoned in that tower and on the brink of being turned into mindless automatons, I couldn't take a risk like that.

So I was going to make someone take a risk for me.

"I'm still not sure I can do what you're asking, Kyle."

I looked to my right. Vortex hovered by my side. She looked concerned. I'd reached out to her individually and asked for this favor. I knew Orion wouldn't sign off a Resistance move like this. Vortex and I saw eye to eye on a lot of things. Besides, I'd saved her life more times than she'd saved mine, so she owed me a favor. "I've seen what you're capable of. I know if you just focus, you'll be able to control his mind."

Vortex shook her head. "It doesn't work like that."

"It doesn't? Or are you just too afraid of what might happen if you push too far?"

Vortex looked me in my eyes. Her ginger hair looked dull, its glow weakened by the stresses of war. "You've no idea what it's like to be in my mind."

"You make people have nightmares. I imagine you're pretty used to seeing horrible things—"

"When I create the nightmares in other people's minds, I have to... I have to let my own demons in. Now I've got to a point where I can just see them in the corner of my mind, locked away. But... but when I try to push further, I have to let them out." Her hands shook. "And I don't know if I can let them out."

Vortex's eyes were wide. She rubbed her arms. I'd never seen her looking this uncomfortable. "What are your demons?" I asked.

She opened her mouth to respond. Then, she closed her lips and shook her head. "They're something I'd rather not talk about right now."

I wanted to push Vortex further, but I respected her decision not to speak. I looked back down at Nycto. He was sat there in his gear, all but his helmet. He looked totally at peace, like he was meditating or something. "We go down there. I pin him down. You get inside his head. And when you're in there, you go back to Saint's tower and you get my people to safety."

"What about everyone else locked up in that place?"

"We deal with them in time. Together."

"And what if... what if I can't do it?"

I put my hand on Vortex's. "You can. I trust you."

For a moment, as Vortex looked into my eyes, I felt warmth inside. Not saying I had a crush or anything like that, but it definitely felt like we had a special kind of friendship. I'd liked Vortex ever since we'd first met. Okay, maybe not since we'd *first* met, since she'd made me see my dead sister in my very first Vortex-induced nightmare. But since then, we'd always got on. We had each other's backs.

"Okay," she said. "I'll try."

I smiled.

We lowered down toward Nycto. The tropical sounds of the stiflingly hot Amazon echoed all around. Something seemed weird about all this. I'd spent so much time tracking Nycto down, and I finally found him sitting silently in the middle of the rainforest? It didn't seem right. It didn't add up.

Then again, when had anything Daniel Septer did ever truly added up?

We descended closer to him. I held on to Vortex's hand, passing my invisibility on to her. I lifted a hand and got ready to freeze Daniel. I wanted to paralyze him with minimal fuss, then Vortex could get on with invading his mind. But I had to play this right.

I was just meters away from him. I held out my hand. Built up a huge ball of ice.

"You ready?" I whispered.

Vortex nodded. Her eyes started to roll back. "Ready."

"I know you're there, idiots."

I heard a blast behind me.

When I looked to my right, Vortex was gone.

"What did you—"

Nycto flew into my chest. He pinned me down on the ground.

I tried to fight back but he covered my mouth. Then, in his hands, a massive fireball grew.

"Shut up and stop fighting."

I kicked back. I tried to teleport away, but my powers felt weakened. I realized then that it's because Nycto had one of those resistance bars around me. An anti-energy band from the tower. He had me, defenseless.

"That's it," he said. "Much better. I prefer it when you aren't being such a drama queen."

"Let me go!"

"Now's not the time to let you go," Nycto said, walking around the right side of me. "Not when we've got so much to discuss."

"There's nothing to discuss. I want my family back. I want my friends back. I want Ellicia back."

"And if you play your cards right, you might get them back."

Nycto's words threw me. I wasn't expecting him to say something like that. "What do... what do you mean?"

He crouched down beside me. I didn't see Nycto anymore. I just saw the skinny face of Daniel Septer. The kid who'd been bullied at school. "You really don't know. Do you?"

I frowned. I realized I'd stopped fighting back. I was just too weak. "Know what?"

A smile stretched across Daniel's face. He held out a hand. "Hello, Kyle. Let me formally introduce myself."

"I know exactly what you are."

Daniel chuckled. He shook his head. "No. No, you don't."

He put a hand in my left hand.

I felt something strange take over me. Like déjà vu.

I'd felt that hand before.

I'd felt those fingers in my hand when...

Nausea welled up inside as a horrifying understanding struck me.

"Get the party balloons out," Daniel said. "It's time we had a family reunion. Brother."

25

*S*ixteen years ago...

JONATHAN HARTSMITH WALKED down the corridor and questioned whether he really wanted to do what he was planning to do.

It was the middle of December. The streets outside were covered in ice. The weather warnings were ordering people to stay at home. Christmas was just around the corner, and nobody wanted to see anyone die in the cold at this time of year.

Jonathan didn't feel cold, though. He'd never felt cold all his life.

Because Jonathan Hartsmith was different.

The dim lights of the clinic flickered as he walked past them. He was used to the lights flickering by now. He'd had to deal with it all his life, after all.

He first knew he was different when he was playing in a paddling pool in his garden. He'd got mad at another kid, Ellen

Halshaw. She'd kept on splashing him and it just made him so mad that he lifted the entire pool of water with his hands, into the air, and covered her in it.

His parents tried denying there was something different at first. But as more and more little moments of weirdness cropped up in his life, Jonathan soon adapted to his reality, as did his mom and dad: he was different. Very different. That was his secret.

It was a secret he'd kept from his loving wife, Eleanor. He didn't want her to see him as a freak. He'd spent his whole childhood convincing himself and the people around him that he was just a normal guy—and failing. As much as he knew Eleanor loved him for who he was, Jonathan still felt like he was holding a major part of himself back from her to protect her.

He walked further down the corridor. Checked the doors. Dr. Woods. Dr. Burza. Dr. Kelvin.

Life between Eleanor and him seemed good. They'd been married eight years back. They had a little girl soon after they first married—Sophie, who was now five. Last year, they'd had a little boy, Michael. And they'd had *another* little boy this year, too. Anthony. Having three kids wasn't easy, sure. It was even harder than you might imagine. But really, Jonathan loved it. He got a real kick from it.

That was until Sophie was diagnosed with terminal leukemia just months back.

He tasted sick in his mouth as he approached the last door on the right. He didn't like to think of Sophie's pain too much. It just made him feel weak and defenseless. He and Eleanor tried everything to help take her pain away, but it wasn't easy. She was a fighter, but she was only a five-year-old kid. Besides, with Michael and Anthony to look after too, it was hard being equally responsible for all three of them.

Never before had Jonathan felt so defenseless.

Then he got a knock on the door.

He'd been expecting a knock for quite a while. It went back to when he'd saved a load of people from a falling aircraft. He'd used his... *abilities* to stop a plane falling in midair. Saved everyone on board. Of course, there was no official confirmation that it was a man who'd done this, but enough conspiracy theories were going around to catch the government's attention.

He stopped in front of the final door. Held his breath.

There wasn't a "Dr" on this door.

Just "Reverend Lewis".

He lifted his hand and knocked on the wooden door.

The knock on the door that he'd got four weeks back had been from a government official. They'd sat down and told him they knew what he was capable of. Somewhere down the line of his ancestors, he must've been born of a man or woman who they'd been testing abilities on ever since the Second World War. But they'd never seen abilities as pure and as refined as Jonathan's. They wanted to take him in to transfer those abilities to others.

Jonathan agreed. He saw what just a trickle of his blood could do. Not everyone was receptive, but the government had developed a technology to figure out whether a person's blood type *was* receptive. After they'd taken several vials of it, they told Jonathan that his blood would be used to create something beautiful. To usher in a new utopia within a matter of years.

Then they told Jonathan they knew of another like him. Another with stunning abilities.

One of those abilities?

He could heal other people.

The door in front of Jonathan opened up.

Standing at the other side of the door was a man. He had short black hair. Big bags under his eyes. He was a little tubby around the waist. His white shirt was creased, and his trousers were too slim for his body. He hardly looked remarkable.

He held out a hand. "Jonathan. Come on in. Pleasure to finally meet you."

Jonathan took his hand. "Reverend Lewis. I've heard a lot about you."

Reverend Lewis waved his other hand then led Jonathan into his office. "You don't have to call me Reverend Lewis. It's a real mouthful. Just Lewis would suffice. Or if you're feeling extra generous, 'Saint.'"

Jonathan sat down opposite Lewis. His office was quaint. There was clutter all over the place. Balls of elastic bands. Drawings of the world. Diagrams filled with equations. A faint sourness of a decaying fruit bowl filled the air.

"Oh, the bananas," Lewis said, noticing where Jonathan was looking. "I always leave them just past their good phase, don't you?"

Jonathan watched as the brown, crinkled bananas turned straight again, and went vibrant yellow.

He looked back at Lewis in amazement. "So your daughter. I'm assuming you want to cut to the chase."

Jonathan nodded. "Sorry. It's just..."

"Meeting someone else with powers like yours for the first time is weird, hmm?"

"Something like that."

"Makes you wonder just how long it'll take before we're not so special at all."

"What do you mean?"

"Those vials of blood. You and I both know what the government plan to do with them."

"I guess. But they could go to good use."

"Perhaps so," Lewis said. There was a sinister look about him, like he wasn't totally present. It snapped away almost as immediately as Jonathan noticed it, though. He clapped his hands together. "Anyway. Your daughter. Where is she?"

"She's... she's at home."

"Well, I'll need her here to—"

"My other children."

Lewis looked down at some paper. "Two boys, I believe."

"I can't have them go through what Sophie's gone through. I can't have them feeling the pain she's felt. Ever."

"You're asking me to cure them before they're ill?"

"I'm asking you to do whatever you can for them."

Lewis shook his head. "It's tough."

"What my daughter's going through is tough."

"It'll require... more than just me. It'll require you, too. A union of our abilities."

Jonathan looked down at the brown carpet. "Whatever it takes."

"You seem apprehensive about something."

He looked back up at Jonathan. "I just want to look out for my children."

"And you are doing," Lewis said. "You're doing exactly that. Now when can we start?"

Two DAYS LATER, Jonathan looked over his children as they hovered over a large pool of water.

His arms were strapped up with tubes. So too were Lewis'.

"And you're absolutely positive there'll be no side effects?"

Lewis shook his head. "I've tried this a million times. From animals to humans. From common colds to cancer. I can heal them. But I'll need your blood too."

Jonathan's mouth was dry. He nodded. Walked over to Sophie and kissed her on her warm head. "Daddy's going to make you better again. I promise."

"I don't like this," Sophie said. She looked around at her brothers beside her, the pool of water below.

"Me neither," Jonathan said. "Me neither."

He kissed his daughter on her forehead then he backed away.

When he was ready, he nodded at Lewis.

He heard the metal bed lower into the water, but he couldn't watch. He understood the risks. He could drown his children right here. He was trusting a man he barely knew to cure everything he cared about.

But if he didn't, what hope did any of them have?

He felt a prick in his arm. Blood ran through the tubes from his veins and into the water.

"Focus your powers," Lewis said, as he stood over the water, which splashed with the kicks of Sophie and the boys. "Put all your powers into making them better again."

Jonathan focused. He thought about the good times he'd had with his children. He thought about the laughs they'd had together. The joy they'd shared. He felt a tear drop down his cheek as he focused his powers further and further, felt the energy slipping out of his body, into his blood, and into that water.

"Good," Lewis said. "That's good."

He kept on pushing even further. The longer it went on, the more splashes he heard, the more Jonathan wanted to stop.

"How long does it—"

"It's almost done," Lewis said.

"How long's almost—"

"Just keep your focus!"

Jonathan resisted every urge in his body telling him to stop this and poured more of his focus into his children. Sophie was going to be okay again. His other children were never going to feel pain again. It was all going to be okay.

He heard the splashing go weak.

Then, it stopped.

He opened his tearful eyes.

"What happened?"

Lewis looked down at the water, wide-eyed.

"I asked you what happened—"

"It's done," he said.

Jonathan looked down into the water and he saw his children lying static.

Their eyes were open.

Beams of light shone from them.

"What have you..."

"They won't remember you now. And they never will. But you can live in reassurance that your children will never get sick. Not anymore. Not now they're like us."

Lewis smiled as he lifted the bed from the water. The light in Sophie's eyes dimmed. When she opened them, she looked around, panicked, spitting up water and phlegm. "Dad?" she said.

Jonathan reached down but she struggled out of his way.

"My dad. Where's my dad? I want my dad."

"I'm here, sweetheart—"

"I want my dad!"

Jonathan looked around at his three children. Children that were like him, now. But children that weren't *his,* not in their minds, not anymore.

"Why have you done this?" he asked.

Lewis smiled. "I wanted to know I could create them. I wanted to know just how far I could take my powers. Now I do... well, they can go off and live their lives. One day, they'll come back to me. When I'm a reverend no more. When I really am a saint."

THREE HOURS LATER, when Jonathan returned home, there was someone sitting at his dining table.

They were holding a warrant for his arrest.

And they were holding a gun like no other he'd ever seen.

It was that moment that he was taken away from his wife, from their children—who were all moved into different homes with fresh memories and completely fresh identities. Even the families they were moved in with had memories implanted in their minds—as if they'd been living a life with those children all along.

It was at that moment that Jonathan became just another experiment. That the government decided he was too strong to have his own will.

It was that day that he became Orion.

The first Hero.

26

"This can't be true. You... You're lying. You have to be lying."

I heard Nycto's words spiraling around my mind, but still they didn't make total sense.

He was my brother.

He stood over me, smile on his face. His hands were on his hips. I didn't see him as "Nycto" anymore. I saw him as Daniel Septer, the human being.

I kept on shaking my head, goose pimples spreading up my skin. "It isn't true. It can't be true."

"And yet now I've told you, you remember. You know it's true. Don't you?"

I shook my head but I couldn't speak. After all, Daniel was right. The memories had flooded back in dramatic fashion.

I felt myself underwater, someone by my side.

I felt water filling my lungs.

And then I saw myself resurfacing from the water feeling an extreme power running through my body. A power that must've been there right from that day, not the day of the Great Blast like I'd first thought. But a power that had only awoken in me when I turned sixteen.

"How... How do you—"

"I'd love to say Saint told me," Daniel said, walking through the tall grass of the rainforest and sitting on a nearby rock. "Truth is, the memories hit me a few days ago. Sudden and sharp. But in a way, it kinda felt like they'd—"

"Always been there," I said.

Daniel smiled and nodded. "You had the dreams too?"

I went to respond but then I saw just how dangerous a game I was playing. "Just because you think you saw something doesn't mean we're cool."

"Hey. We're brothers. We're 'cool' by design."

"I don't think so," I said.

I stood. Walked away. I wasn't sure where I was going, only that I had to get away from here. I had to clear my mind and figure out what I was going to do next. Besides, Daniel had banished Vortex right when we'd been sneaking up on him. If he were all good, he wouldn't have done a thing like that.

"So you're just going to walk away before we've even spoken properly? Before we've had a chance to truly catch up?"

"What more is there to say, really?"

"Well I was hoping we could at least have a brotherly hug."

"You're with Saint. If you're with Saint, that means you're against me."

"I joined Saint because I saw the life humans created for themselves and I didn't want to be a part of that."

"You're just a cog in his game. Don't you see that?"

Daniel ignored my question. "What Saint's trying to do. It could cure the planet's ills for good. Humanity is the virus. I stand by that to this day. It's out of control, and there's only one way to deal with that. Sure, Saint's methods aren't the exact methods I'd use. They're a little... unorthodox."

"Compared to your way," I said. "Attacking the prom venue. Killing Mike Beacon."

Daniel lifted his shoulders. "I am sorry for what happened there. Truly. I was angry. I'd just discovered my powers and I had a point to prove."

"Well, you proved it. You proved it alright."

"And then when you put me down, I was mad. I was filled with vengeance. A vengeance that... that muddied what I was really trying to do."

"Kill everyone on the planet," I said.

Daniel shook his head. "It's not as clear cut as that."

"It looked pretty clear cut to me."

He paused, then hovered a little off the ground. "I made some errors of judgment. But now I see clearly what I must do."

He instantly appeared above me. He held out his hand. For a moment, I thought he was going to fire a ball of fire at me.

But he didn't.

He just kept his hand out.

I frowned. "What is this?"

"This is what I call a hand," Daniel said.

"You know what I'm asking. This. All this. What are you doing?"

Daniel sighed, then crouched down, pulling me to my feet.

I pushed his hands away once we were standing. "Get away from me."

"When I discovered the truth, I saw things clearly for the first time in my life. I saw... I saw what has to happen. What I have to do."

I shook my head. "I don't get what you're saying."

"We're brothers, Kyle. Dammit, our surnames even have the same damned letters."

I took a moment to consider that. Peters. Septer. Shit. He was right. Bit weird, but right.

Daniel stepped closer to me. "I've seen what Saint's doing, firsthand. I've seen what he wants. And while I agree that the planet's out of control at the hands of humans... Kyle, there's something else you need to understand, too. Something about... about that day we were given our powers."

Before Daniel told me the secret, I was confident I'd never come around to his way of thinking. I was certain I'd never be able to trust him.

When he told me the secret, my entire world changed.

"What... what does it mean?" I asked. It was the only thing I could think of. The only words that would leave my lips.

Daniel put a hand on my shoulder. It should've made me feel sick. It should've made my stomach turn. But it didn't.

Instead, it made me feel comfortable.

It made me truly understand.

"You're going to take me back to the Resistance," he said. "You're going to take me to Orion. To our biological father. And then you're going to hear the truth from him. We both are. We both deserve to."

I was so stunned by Daniel's revelation that I couldn't even argue.

"What then?" I asked.

Daniel hovered upwards, and I hovered with him. Underneath, the Amazon got further and further away. "We're going to lead the Resistance into Saint's tower," he said. "And we're going to stop Saint. Before he takes the secret away from us for good."

27

"So, I hope you've got the Resistance ready to roll out a nice welcome party for me."

Just hearing Daniel Septer's voice in my ear reminded me of the stupidity of what I was about to do. "Don't push your luck," I said.

The morning sun shone over the Tanzanian coast. I'd tracked down the Resistance to an island around the Southern Hemisphere. It was a risky find. I knew a lot of islands around this way had fallen already. But before I launched my attack on Saint, there was something I needed to do.

There was something I needed to understand, and as much as I hated to admit it, Daniel deserved an answer just as much as I did.

"Didn't you always dream of this day?" Daniel asked, as we hovered through the skies trying to track down the exact island, the sun beating down on our backs.

"I mighta had a nightmare about it once or twice."

"Don't get me wrong, I'd much rather we were conquering the world together. I mean, I did offer."

"Yeah. Somehow I don't think our goals matched up too well."

"But it's kind of nice," Daniel said, as the breeze brushed our faces. "You've got to admit. Right?"

I didn't admit it, of course. The thought of flying around with someone I was so keen to take down was sickening. I felt like I was in the wrong for even hearing him out. He'd hurt Ellicia. Threatened my entire family.

But he was family. He was the brother I'd never known I'd had.

There was an unshakable bond I just couldn't put my finger on.

"So how exactly do you go about a thing like this?" Daniel asked.

"A thing like what?"

"Taking, you know, one of your arch enemies into your circle of friends. Can't be the easiest of tasks."

I looked down at the island below. I could feel the power radiating from it. "It won't be. But I doubt you'll be sticking around for long."

I shot down toward it. Daniel pulled me back with his powers, a reminder that he was every bit my match.

He smiled. "Maybe I will stick around. Maybe I'll fit right in."

I pushed back with strong powers of my own. "Let's take things one step at a time."

We landed on the island. There was a sandy beach that stretched on for a mile or so. The waves crashed against the shore. The thick trees to our right shook in the breeze, the sounds of wild animals partying within.

Otherwise, it was silent. Empty.

"You sure this is the place?" Daniel asked.

"Yeah. I can feel it. Can't you?"

Daniel glanced down. "Sure, I can feel it. I just—"

"You saying you can't feel it and I can?"

"I didn't mean that."

I shrugged and walked along the beach. I couldn't believe it, but I was actually smiling. "Guess you are the younger brother. Makes sense that your powers won't be quite as sharp."

I felt a sharpness against my neck, like a knife. It stopped me in my tracks.

Daniel was smiling. "Don't talk to me about 'sharp'."

I pushed back against his powers and continued my walk along the beach. I was certain I could feel the presence of the rest of the Resistance around. I'd wanted to be the one to see them first, not the other way around. I didn't want to surprise them. The last time the group had seen me, they'd cut me loose after the escape from Saint's tower. Vortex had seen me since, and the last time we'd been together, Daniel had shot her from the sky. He'd reassured me she was okay, though. He'd just insisted we needed a little time.

"Hold your ground. Don't move a damned muscle."

I heard Stone's voice. I lifted my hands and turned around.

"Hey. I told you not to—"

"We're good. We're not here to hurt anyone."

I saw the amazement in Stone's eyes. Beside him, Ember. Flames sprouted from his hands. "You're walking along the beach with Nycto," he said. "How in the name of hell can you say 'we're good'?"

"Kyle's right," Daniel said. Dammit. I'd been hoping he'd just keep his mouth shut and let me do the talking. He lifted his hands. "We're here totally in peace."

"Well, I obviously am," I said.

"Neither us are going to hurt you."

"Daniel, you don't have to speak for me. They know I'm not gonna—"

"Just shut the hell up," Stone said. "I can't think right now. And when I can't think, I get mad. Real mad. You've seen me when I'm mad, Kyle. You know you're gonna wanna explain what's happening here and calm me down fast if you don't want me to be mad at you."

I looked at the Resistance. All the original crew was here now. Stone. Roadrunner. Ember. Vortex. No sign of Orion, though. "We need to speak to Orion."

"You want to take Nycto to Orion?" Vortex said, holding her face. "That devil teleported me right to the middle of a Texan farm. I got stomped by cattle. Lots of cattle."

"Sorry," Daniel said. "I tried to picture where you'd fit in most. If it was being shat on by a bunch of bulls then hey, that's just how the world works."

Vortex shook her head. Her eyes started rolling back. "I'm not standing for this crap."

"Wait," I said.

"Time for waiting's over, kid," Stone said. His arms covered in hard rock, as did his chest.

Beside him, Ember ignited.

"Get the hell away from here right this second or we'll attack. I swear we'll—"

"Wait!"

Orion walked out from the trees. He was dressed in his usual Bowler gear. The trench coat. The bowler hat. His face was covered. I'd still never seen his face.

"Watch your step, Orion," Ember said. "Nycto's here, and I think he's got into Kyle's head."

"He's not got into my head," I said.

"Which is exactly what you'd say if he'd got into your—"

"What's happening here?" Orion asked. "What is this about?"

The calm way he asked it made me realize he knew. He

understood exactly what this was about. He was just bracing himself to admit it.

I stood with Daniel by my side and I prayed to God he didn't open his big mouth. Now wasn't the time.

"Kyle," he said. "What's... What's this about?"

I swallowed a lump in my throat. I knew now was the time.

"We know," I said. "Both of us know."

Orion looked at us both for a few seconds. Then, he lowered his head.

"Then I think it's time I was completely honest with you both. I think it's time you... you heard it from me."

He turned around and started walking into the forest.

Daniel walked around the back of me, slapped my back.

"Sounds good, Daddy," he said.

I bit my lip and listened to the whispers of shock as they spread through the Resistance, and I walked into the forest toward the news that changed my life forever.

28

Never underestimate just how rapidly your life can change.

I stood beside Daniel Septer—Nycto. Neither of us were fighting, which was a remarkable change in itself. But even weirder than the end to our conflict?

The fact that we were looking at our biological father.

And the fact that our biological father was Orion all along.

"How did any of this happen?" I asked.

Orion hadn't spoken yet. We stood in the middle of the forest. I could hear the splashing of a nearby waterfall as the warm sun beat down on my head. In the distance, I heard the faint chatter of the rest of the Resistance. But they weren't close enough that they were going to be a problem.

"It's a long story that spanned many years."

"And we've got time," Daniel said. "We deserve to hear what happened. Whether the rumors are true."

It felt weird to be stood beside Daniel against Orion. Daniel had threatened to destroy humanity. Orion was the one who'd fought against Saint when destruction seemed inevitable. And now it was me who was standing against Orion; against the true leader of the Resistance.

"When we had you... your mother and I—"

"Who is our mother?" I asked.

"She was called Eleanor. She was a lovely woman."

"'Was'?"

"She died soon after I was taken in for government experimentation. Cancer."

A sickly taste filled my mouth. She was a woman I'd never met and a mother I'd never even known I'd had. And yet it hurt to know that she'd gone. The woman who'd created me and raised me in a life I didn't remember was gone, just like Mom.

"Why didn't you tell us the truth?" I asked.

"Because it wouldn't be fair on me to tell you the truth."

"So instead you thought it was fairer if we just grew up not knowing who our real dad was?"

"I wanted to open up to you both. Believe me, I did. I tried, several times."

"Clearly tried really damned hard."

"But I saw the lives you were living. I saw you were with... good people. Plus, you had memories of your own. I'd look like a madman. You wouldn't believe me. No one would."

Daniel laughed. "You thought I was with good people?"

Orion shook his head. "What happened to you at the hands of your stepfather was regrettable."

"Yeah," he said. "Yeah, it was. What a pity I didn't have, like, one of the most powerful ULTRAs out there as my biological father with the ability to help me... Oh, wait a sec."

I could understand Daniel's bitterness. I didn't know he'd grown up in a bad household, but I knew he got a rough time at school.

"I knew what I was," Orion said. "It scared me. The thought

of us interacting terrified me. Because for all Saint's flaws—and he has many—he never did pursue you."

"So Saint knew who we were all along, too?"

"No. When Saint helped me transmit my powers and his into you... I was taken away, and so too were the pair of you. That was a government decision. You were given new identities, new memories."

"New memories?"

Orion nodded. "Like I said. So too did the people around you."

I couldn't believe what I was actually hearing. It was like something out of a sci-fi movie. Then again, I guess I was like something out of a sci-fi movie, too. "So my family thought I was theirs all along."

"The abilities of the government are amazing and terribly scary. All of us could've lived lives we've no idea actually occurred. But in a way, those changed existences were a blessing in disguise. Because if Saint had known who you were when you were younger, then I dread to think how he might have abused his powers."

All this information was making me dizzy. My chest was tight, and I felt like I couldn't breathe.

"What happened to you... to both of you. I apologize."

"Would you ever have told us who you were if we hadn't found the truth?" Daniel asked.

Orion nodded quickly. "Of course. I would."

"When?"

He didn't respond to that. He just stared into my eyes.

"Your face," I said.

"What?"

"You're our father. And we've never even seen your face."

Orion lowered his head. Then he looked back up at the pair of us. "You won't like what you see."

"I don't care what I see. I just... I just want to see what you look like."

Orion hesitated. Then he lifted his hat from his head, lowered the mask covering his face.

His skin was completely wrinkled. His eyes were just little dots in his skull. It looked like his eyebrows were on the verge of swallowing up his eyes completely.

"You look..."

"Old?" Orion asked.

I shook my head, but he was right. He looked centuries old.

He went to pull his mask back up. "That's what years and years of using abilities like ours does to us. You'd better get used to it. Appreciate your good looks while they last."

I looked into Orion's eyes and for a split second, I saw myself, and I saw Daniel.

"What about the other thing?" Daniel said.

Orion covered his face. "What other thing?"

"The other part of the story. Our... our sister."

Weirdly, I'd been avoiding bringing up that part of Daniel's story simply because I was positive it couldn't be true. And if it was true, then it changed everything.

If it was true, I wasn't sure what to believe about the world anymore.

Orion looked at the ground. There was a detachment to him now he was masked up again. He didn't respond.

"Is it true?" I asked, echoing Daniel.

"Your sister was... She was ill. Very ill—"

"I want to hear you say it. I want to hear it from you."

Orion hesitated again. He looked from me to Daniel and back again. The trees behind rustled, and the rest of the Resistance appeared.

"Everything okay here?" Ember asked.

"We've got 'em if you want 'em dealt with, boss," Stone said.

Orion didn't react to any of the Resistance. He just looked into my eyes, and I knew the rumor was true already.

"Kyle, I... I don't know how to tell you this. But your sister. Cassie. She was your biological sister. And she didn't die in the Great Blast at all."

29

E*ight Years Ago...*

ORION WATCHED the funeral from afar and he knew he needed to act fast.

Rain lashed down from the thick gray clouds above. He stood behind the church, completely exhausted, but knowing full well he needed to watch himself if he wanted to get out of here alive. He was risking everything by being here in the first place. But he couldn't just walk away. Not when he knew the truth about Cassie, or Sophie, as he called her.

His daughter.

He saw them lowering the coffin. By the side of it, his son's new parents. They looked filled with grief. Orion had always thought they were doing a good job with his biological children. Then again, they would be. Apparently, the government had imprinted some kind of memories into them so that they were convinced they'd had these kids themselves. It worked out better that way, for their own protection.

He watched as young Kyle, as he was now called, walked up to the side of his sister's grave and threw a flower down toward her. Orion could tell just from the look in his eyes that he didn't really understand what was happening here. This was so cruel. He wanted to tell this family the truth.

But telling them the truth just meant more danger for his daughter, more danger for his entire family.

He waited for the families to depart before making his move.

Then, he put his bowler hat on that he'd found back home lying around the direst depths of his makeshift apartment and he walked to the grave.

He stopped by its side. Just looking down and seeing that small coffin made him want to throw up. He wiped his eyes. Sure, her name had been changed, but this girl was still his daughter. He had flashbacks to the day she'd been taken away from him. The day he'd given up a piece of himself to save her life and heal her.

Only he'd passed his powers on to all his children.

That was why he was thankful for the government. They'd taken all his children away and given them whole new identities. They were now Cassie, Kyle, and Daniel.

Saint didn't know about Kyle and Daniel, but he knew about "Cassie" somehow. The government had made a bold move keeping her and Kyle together. Perhaps it was a way of throwing those who might be out for them. He couldn't be sure. It certainly seemed to have fooled Saint, as he hadn't gone after Kyle.

But "Cassie" was still in danger.

Orion looked around the churchyard. All of the cars had departed. The rain lashed down heavier. It looked clear.

He lowered down toward the coffin.

He put his hands on top of it. Focused on the stiff locks that held his daughter inside.

Then he heard chatter above.

He held his breath and activated his invisibility.

He heard the footsteps pass by. The voices diminished.

As soon as he was sure they'd gone, he returned his focus to the coffin.

He felt the latches breaking. Part of him didn't want to open this lid and see his daughter lying there so peaceful. But he knew he had to. After all, she didn't die. Not right away. That was part of the "healing" process that Saint treated her to back when he was Reverend Lewis. She had seven days, he'd said. Seven days of living in a deathlike state, only wake-able by the powers of an ULTRA.

Today was the sixth day.

Orion pulled away the coffin lid and held his breath. It wasn't going to be easy looking his daughter in the eye. She'd probably be confused. And he knew he couldn't exactly take her back to her family. There'd be too many questions, and the answers would put her and her brother in danger.

He had to get her somewhere safe. Somewhere no one would find her.

He closed his eyes. Took a deep breath.

Then he lifted the coffin lid completely.

He stared down into it for a few seconds, maybe longer. He couldn't understand what he was looking at. It didn't make sense.

But then he saw the note, and it added up completely in a horrible, sinister fashion.

The coffin was empty.

Lying on the white padding, a note.

Orion lifted the note with a shaking hand. He'd thought

he'd dealt with Saint. He'd thought he'd put him somewhere he wouldn't come back from. And maybe he had, but with the last of his unstoppable powers, he'd seen to one final act.

Too late, the note read.

SOMEWHERE FAR AWAY, with the last of his crippled powers, Saint lowered Orion's daughter into the ground.

He shouldn't be here. His physical form was stuck in a limbo that Orion had cast him into.

But with the last of his powers, he'd seen to one thing. A thing that was going to be very, very important when he finally got his strength back.

Which he would.

"You rest now, my angel," Saint said, as he lowered a sleeping—but living—girl into the ground. He'd woken her so she survived, but he'd soon put her back to sleep again. She needed a long rest now. "You won't know a thing until the day comes to wake you."

He closed the lid of her coffin.

Then he disappeared into that dark void Orion had cast him into, waiting for the day his powers recharged.

EIGHT YEARS LATER, Saint lifted the coffin lid and smiled.

"Come on now, my angel. It's time for you to wake."

Cassie opened her eyes.

30

"You lied to me. All this time... All these years. You lied to me."

When I spoke the words, I could sense the look of shame behind Orion's masked face. Daniel stood beside me, not saying a word. The rest of the Resistance were behind us now too, many of them learning the truth not only of Orion's connection to Daniel and me, but the truth about my sister.

"I wanted to tell you," Orion said.

"If you'd wanted to tell me you'd have told me."

"You have to see how dangerous it—"

"You let me and my family believe my sister was dead!"

My shout made the leaves shake from the trees. My voice echoed for miles. My chest tightened, like it was in the grasp of a vice grip. I wasn't sure how much longer I could control my anger.

"You let me and my mom and dad believe Cassie was dead all that time."

"I thought it was for the best."

"For the best?" I walked closer to Orion, my fists tightening.

I couldn't stop the electric ice radiating through my body. "It broke my parents down. It—it nearly killed my dad."

"And for that I'm sorry. Truly."

"You're sorry? Really? That's all you have to say?"

Orion looked down at the ground. He looked the most defeated I'd ever seen him.

"As long as you're sorry, I suppose everything's alright."

"What did I tell you, Kyle?" Daniel said. There was a slight smile on his face which irritated me. "Orion isn't the good guy he claims to be."

"Shut up. Seriously, just shut up. I don't need to hear from you right now."

Daniel raised his hands. "Don't shoot the messenger."

I squeezed the bridge of my nose. I felt sick and dizzy. All of this was too much to take in right now. "So Cassie. If... If she had abilities too. If she's still alive. Then where is she?"

Orion didn't respond right away, which immediately set the alarm bells ringing.

"Orion? The least you can do is be straight with me about—"

"I don't know where she is."

"What?"

"Your sister. I don't know where she is."

Those six words hit me the hardest of all. "What do you mean you don't know where she is?"

"When I went to pull her from her... from her grave. She was already gone."

"Then who took her?"

Orion looked past me and at the Resistance. "It's time we started planning our next–"

"Who took her?"

He looked at me again. Surely by now he saw there was no dodging my questions. "I think Saint took her."

I squeezed my fists together and felt the anger burning under my skin. I needed to get to Saint more than ever now. I needed to make him pay for what he'd done.

"Kyle, wait."

"No," I said. "You don't get to tell me to wait anymore."

I closed my eyes and pictured Saint's tower. I couldn't think properly, but I knew it was where I had to be right now.

"We can fight back against Saint, but only together. If you go flying in there alone, you're risking throwing away everything."

"I don't care about anything else."

"She's my daughter too, remember."

There was something to those words that made me tone down my anger. There was a fragility to Orion's voice that connected with me.

When I grounded myself back on the island in the middle of that forest, I focused on Orion's mask. I could tell that he was shaking.

"Don't you think I've tried to get her back all these years? She... She's my daughter. A daughter I had taken away from me all because of..." He raised his hands, and two balls of energy sprouted from his palms. "All because of this."

His voice cracked now. He sounded exhausted, like his strong front had finally worn away.

"And you are my children, too. Both of you." He looked from me to Daniel and back again. "All these years I've had to watch from the sidelines as you've grown up. All I've wanted all this time is to put my arm around your shoulders and tell you how much I..."

He turned away, his voice failing him completely.

Then he looked back at me.

"I'm sorry for letting you down. I'm sorry for all of this mess. Truly. But the only way we're going to win this battle and the only way we'll ever find out what truly happened to Soph... to Cassie, is if we work together, step by step. No more recklessness."

I let Orion's words sink in. All around me, I heard silence but for the tumbling waterfall.

"I will fight to take down Saint," I said. "I won't hold off anymore. I'll attack stronger than ever. But it's not because of some duty to you or to the Resistance. It's not my way of saying I forgive you. It's because Saint has my friends. He has my girlfriend. He has my dad. The man who's brought me up. My real dad. And I'm fighting because I owe him, big time. I'm fighting because I want to save the lives of the people I care about. Not because of anything else."

Orion lowered his head. I knew the "real dad" thing was a bit of a low blow. After all, Orion hadn't really been able to help the fact he couldn't reach out to me. But he'd let me think my sister was dead when really she was... well, maybe still dead. He'd taken away the hope from my family and sent my dad into a depressive spiral. Worst of all, Mom had died never knowing the truth about Cassie. I couldn't just forgive him for that.

"And I'll fight with you," Orion said. There was a certainty and self-assurance to his voice again now like he'd reapplied his mask. "To the end."

I nodded. Then I looked around at the rest of the Resistance, who glared at Daniel—Nycto—like he was still the enemy. "Then we'd better get a plan together."

31

"This isn't going to be easy. Hell, it's going to be the toughest thing we've ever done in our lives. But we're ULTRAs. So we're made of tough stuff. We can do this if we band together. Okay?"

I spoke as loud as I could to the crowd of the Resistance watching me. We were on the beach. The sun was setting, but we were not turning in tonight. Instead, we were launching the first stage of our fight back.

"Now I know I've said in the past we should just launch our attack on Saint's tower. But now I see we can't just do that. Instead, we need to start winning territory. We need to make Saint *feel* like we're fighting for the cities, and that he's one step ahead. And that's when we launch the attack on his tower."

"So winning back the cities is just a bluff?" Ember asked.

"Not a bluff," I said. "We win back the cities and take the people we rescue there. We protect those cities when Saint strikes against them. That's when we use our opportunity to take the tower and take Saint down."

"How can you be so sure Saint's gonna just let us fly up there into his tower, kid?" Stone asked.

I looked to my right. Daniel stood beside me. "Because I've seen how he works."

All eyes turned on Daniel. I saw heads shaking. Heard whispers.

"And we're supposed to trust *you*?" Stone asked.

"I know there's not a lot of trust here, but what Daniel says makes sense. Saint's tough, but he's shown his weakness many times already. He likes to be at the front of a battle. He likes to be the one to lead his ULTRAbots to glory."

"But how's that gonna help us take down Saint if we're in his tower?"

I looked at Daniel. Instead of letting him speak, I spoke for him considering very few of the Resistance were keen on trusting him. "There's a room in there. A place where Saint sets his ULTRAbot targets. If we can start fighting back for a city, and we can draw Saint and his ULTRAbots to that position, we can send the rest of his ULTRAbots out there to destroy themselves. And destroy Saint."

Vortex shook her head. "I'm not sure I like the sound of this."

"Me neither," Ember said.

"Yeah, make that three," Stone said. "Sounds damned speculative to me."

Orion hadn't spoken since our standoff in the forest. I could tell he was weighing up the situation, figuring out the best way to progress.

"I know it's not going to be easy," I said.

"It's not the taking the city I'm too worried about," Ember said. He was looking right at Daniel. "It's trusting him."

I looked at Daniel. It didn't help that he always had that cocky smile, like he was enjoying the controversy he was causing. "Kyle and I are brothers. Orion over there, he's my daddy. Why would I do a thing to put either of them at risk?"

"Because of your psychopathic tendencies?" Vortex said.

Daniel chuckled. "I'm a lot of things but a psychopath is absolutely not one of them."

"Yeah," Stone said, tensing his fists so they turned to rock. "Ain't that what a psycho would say?"

"Look," I said. "You don't have to trust Daniel. Neither of us has to trust each other. We just have to believe that what we're doing is the best way to take down Saint."

"And if this ULTRAbot targeting thing is bullshit?" Ember said. "If there's no way of turning the ULTRAbots against themselves? What then?"

I swallowed a hard lump in my throat and glanced into Daniel's eyes once more. "Then we do what we've always done. We fight."

I looked around at the Resistance. There were still whispers and grumbles of discontent. I knew it was going to be hard to win them over to fighting by Daniel's side.

"I—"

"I know many of us haven't got off to the best of starts," Daniel said, cutting me short. "But you have to remember that I saved many of you. I freed you from Area 64."

"Yeah," an ULTRA, who was part of the Resistance with fire-red hair, said. "Only for your own gain."

"That was before," Daniel said. "But the truth is, you are my kind. I want to fight alongside my kind."

"And when we win?" Stone shouted. "When Saint's out of the way? You really telling us you ain't just gonna go for another power grab?"

"No he isn't," I said. "Because we aren't going to let him."

Daniel smirked at me. I could understand the skepticism about his motivations. But hell, he was my brother, and I couldn't help but believe he'd seen the right way. We can't choose our family, after all.

"What's in it for you?" Vortex asked. "Truthfully."

Daniel narrowed his eyes. "Why don't you look into my mind and find out?"

Vortex's eyes started to go bloodshot. "Don't try me."

"Okay," I said, eager not to start World War Four right here. "Can we just please have a serious discussion about—"

"What's in it for me?" Daniel said. "Finding out the truth about what happened to my older sister. And punishing the monster who took her away from me."

Daniel's words sounded purer and more convincing than anything else he'd said. It was like he was opening up at last, revealing his true soul.

The disgruntled whispers and murmurings stopped. Instead, I saw the Resistance all looking back at me.

"Whatever happens, wherever we stand, we need to fight," I said.

Many of the Resistance nodded.

"We need to battle to win back territory. Draw Saint out. And then we strike him right in his heart."

More nods. More agreement.

"Are we ready to battle?" I shouted.

"Yeah!" The Resistance called.

"Good," I said. I looked up into the sky. "We've got New York to win back."

[32]

S aint looked around the room filled with humans and he
couldn't shake the smile from his face.

There were so many of them now. And acquiring
them had been so simple. They'd pulled a group of them from
the cities and towns using the ULTRAbots, brought them in
here and put them under a peaceful sleep.

Most of them were still down in the cities, imprisoned by
the ULTRAbots. But they were just part of the next phase.

Saint liked standing amongst these people in the total
silence. It brought him solitude. So when he heard footsteps
echoing through the room, he couldn't help feeling a little agitation creep in.

"What is it?"

He looked around and saw Panther approaching. "News
from the outside," he said.

"Good news or bad news?"

"Depends on your perspective. We're hearing talk that the
Resistance are planning an attack on New York."

Saint felt a smile tug even harder at his cheeks. He'd been
waiting for the Resistance to launch their first major attack for a

long, long time. He knew why they'd do it, of course. They were hoping to catch him off guard, battle their way into the tower to free humanity from its inevitable fate. It was quite cute, in a way. It was all working out so neatly. "That sounds like things are working in our favor."

"Hearing more talks of humans resisting the brainwashing," Panther said. "People just seem to be too tough in places."

"Hmm," Saint said. He had to admit, that was disappointing news. Brainwashing humanity and turning them into his slaves was a key part of his plan for taking the planet completely. Soon, everything would fall in line with what he wanted. Nothing that happened on this earth would happen without his approval. He wanted to control everything, right down to the plants in the ground, the turn of the seasons. Only when he got total control would he be truly satisfied.

"We need to ramp up the brainwashing program if we want to hit our target of total control within the next month."

Saint scratched the back of his neck. The irritation and impatience gnawed at him. He wanted to get his control done with and hit his target, but he knew he couldn't maintain control if he didn't ramp up the power of his brainwashing program.

And that's where the battle for New York would fall right into place. He just needed to train himself to be more patient and let it all happen naturally. This was how he'd planned for it to all unfold. He couldn't get edgy when everything was working out better than he could imagine.

"There's more news," Panther said. He looked at the floor now. "From the Resistance. Kyle... Kyle and Daniel know. About Orion."

That news sparked a joy inside Saint that completely overshadowed any nerves he'd had before. Kyle and Daniel finally knew the true identity of Orion. That was perfect. It meant that Daniel had seen the memory cache he'd left lying around, waiting for him to look at. Memory caches were powerful things, something only the greatest ULTRAs—like himself—could create.

It also meant they knew the truth about their sister.

Well. Not the whole truth.

"Very good," Saint said. "Then you know what you have to do."

Panther looked at Saint for a few seconds like he wasn't totally certain. "Are you sure?"

"Take as many ULTRAbots as possible to New York. Get them ready to fight."

"What about the ULTRAs?"

"Kyle and Daniel must live until they make it here. The rest... rounding them up would be preferable. But as long as we have Kyle and Daniel, do not worry about killing them. There's no use for them in the long term. Except one. He could come in handy."

Saint didn't have to name the ULTRA he referred to for Panther to understand.

He put a hand on Panther's shoulder. "We're very close to something beautiful. I'm thrilled you've chosen to stick around to see the fireworks."

Panther nodded. "I'm completely in service to you."

"And you've been truly excellent."

One moment, Panther had light in his eyes.

The next, the life drifted from his body completely.

He hit the ground. Saint stood over him, then lifted him through the door into that dark corridor where she was waiting. He made sure the power stayed inside Panther's body. It was important he kept that. After all, it was the very food that helped her control the minds of the humans.

He stood outside the glass window. Held up Panther's body. "Your next meal, my lady."

Nothing but darkness behind the window. No movement whatsoever.

Then, a blue light.

It drifted out of the room. Swooped inside Panther's body. It hovered over it for a few seconds, pulling something away.

And then the light beamed out of this corridor and Saint knew somewhere in the hangar where the humans rested, one—or more—awoke.

He looked into the eyes of the girl behind the glass as she harvested more of the ULTRA powers. Soon, he wouldn't need to feed her at all. Soon, her brother would be beside her, similarly mind washed, and the joint connection of their powers would be enough to brainwash every single human on this planet, whether they were in this tower or living on the ground.

He smiled at the girl. Her hair still looked as shiny as the day he'd pulled her from that coffin and trapped her. Her eyes were still as beautiful as when he'd woken her up to another life. A life in service to him.

Soon, Cassie and Kyle would have their family reunion.

33

I looked down at New York and felt sadness fill my body.

New York was the city I knew better than any other. I'd grown up there, on Staten Island. I'd taken so many trips to Manhattan, and even though I'd never been a big fan of crowds, I was always amazed by the buzz of people. It always reminded me just how alive the world really was.

New York had never looked deader than it did right now.

Smoke plumed up from the wrecked skyscrapers. Abandoned yellow cabs lined the streets. Horses still pulled carriages ran around the overgrown Central Park, free from the monotony of tourist rides. The billboards of Times Square were completely vacant.

However, it wasn't totally empty. There were movements down in the shadows. I knew what those movements were. We all knew what those movements were.

The ULTRAbots. The ones we were going to fight to take New York back.

"So how exactly do we take a city that doesn't have much left to take?" Ember asked.

I swallowed a lump in my throat. Looked down at the ULTRAbot below me. "Like this."

I slammed my hands together and crashed down into the ULTRAbot. I made sure it was definitely an ULTRAbot and not a brainwashed human—as much as I realized I was going to have to fight some of them, I still didn't like the idea of attacking humans so much.

Then I punched it in the face and knocked its electronic head off.

The second I took down the first ULTRAbot, more of them appeared around me like bees protecting their nest.

"Now's the time to think about fighting!" I called.

Above, the Resistance swooped down and blasted at the ULTRAbots.

I fought back against them, one by one. I fired ice into the face of one. Another one grabbed my leg, twisted it to the point of breaking, so I teleported behind it and fried its mechanics with one of its colleague's bullets.

I saw Stone punching the life out of another of the ULTRAbots. I saw Vortex, Ember, Orion, and Roadrunner all fighting their own ULTRAbots, and the rest of the Resistance fighting their battle, too.

By my side, I saw Daniel. He charged up the flames in his hands and slammed the balls of energy right into the faces of two ULTRAbots, knocking them out of the sky in a flash. If I had any doubts about which side he was on, I knew the truth now.

I started growing wary when I saw the skies were still empty.

"Aren't the others supposed to be heading our way about now?" Ember asked.

"Just keep the faith," I said, as I fired a few more shots of ice at some oncoming ULTRAbots. "Just—"

A strong fist slammed across my face. I felt the powers drift from my body and fell down toward the ground. I knew what'd happened. I'd been hit by one of those paralyzing ULTRAbot bullets. It was lucky I'd put my defenses up at the last second, or I was confident I wouldn't have a face right now.

But I was falling. That wasn't good news for anyone.

I flew into the ground. A crater formed around me. I twisted onto my back and gritted my teeth.

Above, I saw an ULTRAbot holding a gun to my head.

I tried to activate my powers but I was weak. The paralyzing blast had taken it out of me. The rest of the ULTRAs above me were all in battle.

I spat out some blood and held my breath as I waited for the bullet.

The gun charged up.

Then a hole blasted in the ULTRAbot's chest.

I jumped out of the way before the ULTRAbot's bullet could hit me. When I looked past the ULTRAbot, I realized what'd happened.

Daniel was hovering behind it. Two orange spheres of energy rested in his hands. He watched the ULTRAbot fall to its knees and he smiled.

I nodded. "Thanks."

"Was that Kyle Peters, the great Glacies, just thanking me right then?"

"Alright, alright. Don't rub it in."

"Man, allow me my moment."

"You kind of owed me after I kept you alive at the bottom of Krakatoa."

Daniel tutted. "I'd hardly say this makes us even."

Right as he spoke, I heard a humming sound rip through the sky. New York went dark in an instant. I knew why it had to be.

Saint.

But when I focused above, I couldn't see Saint.

I could, however, see masses of ULTRAbots. More than I'd ever seen in my life.

All of them were hurtling down to New York.

"This is it," Daniel said. "We have to get out of here now. We won't get a better chance."

I looked at Orion, Ember, Roadrunner, Vortex and Stone. I looked at the rest of the Resistance fighting alongside them. "But there's too many of them—"

"They chose to fight for you, brother. They chose this path. But we can't be here. Not if we want to save everyone. Okay?"

I watched the ULTRAbots get closer and I knew Daniel was right. Sure, I wanted to go up there and get my revenge against Saint. But another part of me wanted to look Saint in the eye when I got that revenge. Another part of me wanted to be here for this battle.

"Then let's go," I said. "Now."

I started to elevate toward the sky when I heard a blast erupt through the middle of the street.

I looked across and saw a mass of ULTRAbots all around Stone. They held on to him. Dragged him into the sky. More of the ULTRAbot army hurried down, attacked Orion, Ember, Vortex, Roadrunner, the rest of the Resistance. There were way too many to deal with.

"Now, Kyle," Daniel said. "We have to go now!"

I looked at Daniel. Then I looked back at Stone.

The ULTRAbots were all around him.

His punches were weakening.

He was disappearing...

34

I watched the ULTRAbots surround Stone.

"Kyle!" Daniel shouted. "We need to get to Saint's tower right this second!"

I heard Daniel's voice and knew time was running out. All around me, the assault of the ULTRAbots was getting stronger. There were so many of them, more than I'd ever seen in one place. They fought around the burned-out skyscrapers in the New York skyline; the Resistance battled them atop the Empire State Building, the Rockefeller, over Central Park. The air was warm from the heat of explosions.

And in front of me, a group of the ULTRAbots swarmed Stone.

"There's no time," Daniel shouted, dodging the attack of three oncoming ULTRAbots, which fired down at him. "We— we have to move. Right now."

Daniel was right. I knew that much. But I couldn't just let the Resistance fall. These ULTRAs had given up everything to back my plan. The least I could do was fight for them. "We can't go," I said.

Daniel narrowed his eyes. "What?"

I charged up the ice in my hands, tensing my fists. "I can't let the Resistance just fall."

"We knew there'd be casualties. We all agreed there'd be casualties."

I turned around and looked back at the ULTRAbots swarming Stone. "I'm through with casualties."

I fired a blast of ice right into the surrounding crowd.

Just before the ice hit them, I felt time slow down. I saw my ice slipping between the ULTRAbots, worming its way in front of them. Then, when I was sure there was an icy wall between the ULTRAbots and Stone, I dragged my hands out.

The ULTRAbots flew away from Stone like there'd been an explosion in the middle of them. Time sped up again, and they blasted far away, through the sky, some of them right across the city.

In the middle of where they'd surrounded, I saw Stone.

He was still. Rocks crumbled down from his broken body. His eyes were closed, and he was dropping down to the ground below.

"Stone!"

I hovered over to him, blasting aside a few ULTRAbots in the process.

"Kyle, there's no time—"

"Then you go!" I shouted.

Daniel's eyes were wide. For the first time in a long time, I thought he actually looked concerned. "I can't take Saint's tower myself."

"Then you wait for me. You help us fight. Then we go."

"That wasn't the plan. The plan was to turn Saint's ULTRAbots against him."

"I don't see Saint anywhere," I said. "He's—he's sent his heavy artillery, but he isn't here."

More concern on Daniel's face. "I'm sure he's here somewhere."

"Yeah, well, it doesn't look like it. So I'm not just going to leave my people here to die."

I grabbed Stone and hovered in the air. He was heavy in my arms, almost twice my width, but I kept hold of him there in the sky.

"Stone, please," I said. "You... you and I haven't always seen eye to eye. But we can't lose you. We need you. You're strong."

"Um, Kyle," Daniel said.

I ignored him. Kept my focus on Stone. I put my hand on his stony chest, which crumbled to the touch. "You've fought this much. You can keep on fighting. You're one of the strongest ULTRAs I've ever met. Don't give up now. Please."

"Kyle, seriously."

I was about to see what Daniel wanted when Stone opened his eyes and spluttered up dust.

"Whoa," I said, patting his chest, unable to shake the smile from my face. "That's it. That's just it. Cough it right up."

"Bastard," he muttered. "B—bastard."

"That's right. 'Bastard.' You get it all off your chest."

I held on to Stone as the city collapsed around me. I was finally about to see what Daniel wanted when something caught my eye.

Over in the distance, I saw Saint's cloud.

I felt my fists tense. The urge to face him, head on, was stronger than ever. I knew it wasn't the plan, but I'd always liked the idea of taking him down personally while we were head to head. Turning his ULTRAbots against him to do the dirty work? It didn't have the same oomph to it.

But then again, I knew what the plan was. I could hear the sounds of battle and see the explosions all around me as the Resistance and the ULTRAbots came head to head. I had to stick to the plan. I had to hold off fighting Saint right now because that wasn't the plan.

Maybe now I knew Saint was here, the initial plan would work.

But I wasn't going anywhere while I knew the ULTRAbots still had the odds stacked in their favor.

I hovered away from Stone, who'd regained his composure. I looked up at the swathes of ULTRAbots covering the sky above me. There was no sign of Daniel. I wasn't sure what to make of that. Really, I couldn't blame him. I just hoped he was back here when the time was right.

"Kyle. You not supposed to be outta here?" Ember flew to my side. Soon after, Vortex and Orion joined him.

I looked up at the ULTRAbots flying down at us. I tightened my grip and felt the ice sprouting from my fists. "Not until I know you're safe."

"But you have a job to do. You have to take down—"

Ember didn't finish speaking.

Well, he might've. But I didn't hear him.

A burst of energy blasted into my chest. A splitting pain cracked through my skull. I fell down rapidly into the buildings below. All of them fell down toward me.

I twisted around, the taste of blood thick in my mouth. There was a hole in my chest. I had to heal it or I'd die. I had to hurry, or I'd...

I was about to focus on healing myself when an ULTRAbot pulled aside the building and flew at me.

Behind it, another twenty, thirty, forty, all of them pointing their guns, all getting ready to blast me from the face of existence.

35

When you're lying on the ground under a bunch of falling skyscrapers with a hole in your chest, you know you're pretty much screwed.

Oh, and when a bunch of ULTRAbots are closing in on you, giving you zero chance to heal the gaping wound that's on the verge of killing you? Yeah. You're very goddamned screwed.

I looked up at the mass of ULTRAbots above. They all had their guns primed and pointed them at me, ready to fire. Usually when I was in this kind of situation, I'd find a way to use my powers to blast them out of my line of sight. But the pain in my chest was too strong. I was getting weaker by the second. I had to focus on healing myself, or I'd die.

The problem with focusing on healing myself? It might just kill me anyway.

I looked down at my chest. The bitter taste of blood was on my lips. I could hear the droning sounds of battle above and hoped my ULTRAs were okay. I hoped wherever they were, the Resistance was giving the ULTRAbots all they had.

The ULTRAbots hovered lower toward me. I was surprised they hadn't shot me by now, in truth. It seemed weird. They had a golden opportunity to deal with me, put me down, and they were letting the seconds tick by.

And every second that ticked by, I used it as a bonus. I focused on my chest. Healed the broken tissue. Shit, if I'd taken a blast a little further to the left, my heart would've been ripped apart.

Could even *I* bounce back from something like that?

I certainly didn't want to take my chances.

The healing process was agonizing. I bit my lip and tasted even more blood. I winced every time a small piece of tissue was healed, as the muscle regenerated, as my skin healed over. Even I was surprised by the sheer strength of my powers when I was in as dire a situation as this.

Still, the ULTRAbots weren't firing.

I felt myself getting weaker the more of my powers I put into healing. I wondered if this was one of those moments Orion spoke about. The ones that took so much strength that it completely wounded an ULTRA. If it did, then I'd never take down Saint. I'd never be able to lead the ULTRAs again. I'd be totally lost.

But then the skin on my chest healed over.

The ULTRAbots hovered above me.

I looked up at them, into their staring eyes.

"What?" I shouted, stumbling to my feet. "What are you waiting for?"

They held their guns. I thought I saw something in their eyes, then. A glimmer of confusion, like they were caught in two minds about what to do. They were trained to hunt down ULTRAs, so that concerned me.

If they weren't hunting me down, then who was giving that order?

"What are you waiting for?"

I listened to my voice echo around the crater. Rubble

tumbled down as my voice bounced against it. Up above, I saw a glimmer of light where the city of New York stayed engaged in battle.

Then the ULTRAbots' stares focused.

They lifted their guns higher. Tensed on the trigger.

I closed my eyes.

I heard a blast above. It cracked through the rubble and sent more debris falling down in my direction.

It was a blast of orange energy that slammed into the backs of half of the ULTRAbots, disabling them in an instant.

I stood. Flew up at the ULTRAbot nearest to me. I crashed into its chest, knocked it back up toward the ceiling of rubble. It pressed back against me, squeezed my hands. And as I tried to take it down, ice spreading across my hands, I saw that look of confusion once more. The ULTRAbot was caught in two minds about what it wanted to do. Why?

I heard more explosions around me. More balls of energy hit the ULTRAbots. More of them fell down. And above, I saw the rubble falling. The sky appearing. Only it wasn't as full of ULTRAbots anymore. Many of them had fallen.

I went to punch my fist into a final ULTRAbot when a massive rock hit my side.

It knocked me down. I felt myself flying below and prepared for it to crush my head.

Only I stopped.

So too did the rock.

I looked around. Tried to figure out what'd happened.

It was only when I looked above that I realized Daniel was the one keeping me hovering.

He moved the rock away from me. Then he moved the ULTRAbots below it. His eyes were bright, and his body was shaking.

Then he threw the rock down at the ULTRAbots, crushing them in an instant.

His eyes became normal. "Okay. So now we're even?"

I flew up toward him. Together, we looked across the city of New York. The ULTRAbots were lowering in number. Saint was nowhere to be seen.

"So that's Plan A down the crapper," Daniel said.

I looked down at my chest. It was completely healed over. And it dawned on me that maybe I really was a lot stronger than I thought. I knew I was *strong*... but the way I'd actually healed myself when I was in such immediate danger. It made me understand I could use that power and strength even more.

"We don't need Plan A," I said, not anymore.

I flew up into the gray sky. A few ULTRAbots still hovered around, but enough for the Resistance to deal with.

"Where you going?"

I turned around. "We're going to Saint's tower. We're going to face him directly. Then we're going to stop all this mess once and for all."

[36]

When I saw Saint's tower in the distance, I couldn't help the knotting sensation in my stomach.

There was a dark cloud all around, the kind that followed Saint wherever he went. Below, the waves were strong and rapid. If any normal person swam in there, they'd be lost to the sea in an instant. The smell of saltwater was strong in the air, its taste covering my lips. I could hear the gradual hum of something in the distance; the sound of life, as Saint's human brainwashing program powered on. My chest still stung from the blast I'd taken through it not long ago, but I was fine. It still amazed me that I'd survived that blast. Again, it made me realize I was probably stronger than I'd first thought.

"So what's the plan, Einstein?"

I looked to my right. Daniel hovered beside me. He was dressed up to his neck in his Nycto gear, but his mask wasn't in place. Truth be told, I'd still been skeptical about him even when we'd stood together and waited for the ULTRAbots to attack New York. But after he'd helped me fight out of the rubble of the fallen skyscrapers, and after he'd carried on with my new plan to attack Saint's tower head on, my faith in him was growing. My lust for vengeance was falling. I saw the truth clearer than ever before. I needed to protect humanity and ULTRAs from Saint because Saint was evil. Sure, I wanted to get my own revenge on Saint for what he'd done to the people I loved, for those he'd taken away from me. But there was more to it than that. Taking Saint down was a goal in itself. It didn't need to have my own lust for vengeance behind it.

But still, it'd be an absolute treat if I could be the one to put a stop to his era of chaos.

"We can both turn invisible, right?"

"Well, yeah," Daniel said. "But if you think that's gonna get us past Saint's ULTRAbots, you're very wrong."

"It might not get us past the ULTRAbots, but I've... I don't know about you, but I've felt something more recently. A stronger power than I thought I had growing inside me."

"Sounds like a crackpot theory to me."

"Just... Just hear me out. When we were locked in Saint's cells... when the ULTRA called Controlla came to get into my head... I found a way to reverse his powers and turn them against him. It made me wonder if I could do more than I'd been giving myself credit for."

"You give yourself enough credit as it is. You'd be insufferable if you gave yourself anymore."

I ignored Daniel. "And back when you helped me from the ULTRAbots in New York. I had a hole in my chest. I should've died. Hell, I know I can heal myself, but even I shouldn't have been able to bounce back from that."

"So what you're saying is... No. I really don't know what you're saying."

"I'm starting to think that the more danger we're in, the more powerful our powers become. When I put you at the bottom of Krakatoa—"

"Cheers for the reminder."

"Just listen, please. When I buried you there, I put every single damned effort into making sure you'd stay at the bottom of that volcano."

"Thanks for that."

"I tried, but you must've wanted to get out more than anything else."

"Surviving is always a wise priority when you've got a flood of lava heading toward you, sure."

"So you found it in yourself to fight. And sure, it weakened you for a while. It took the energy out of you. But you did it. I'm starting to think maybe we could use that strength to get inside, get past Saint's ULTRAbots and take him down, head on."

Daniel shook his head. "Even if it *did* work, there's no getting past the barriers Saint has in place. They repress our powers. There's definitely no teleporting inside his office and being done with it."

"I'm not sure that's totally true," I said.

Daniel hovered in front of me. He looked right into my eyes. "I'm still not really sure what you're actually suggesting here."

I looked down at the waves below. Watched them bash against each other.

"Kyle?"

"If I go in there. If I... If I throw everything I have into getting in there, alone. I might fail. If I do, I want you to go in there and... I want you to go in there and be the one to take Saint down."

I looked into Daniel's eyes. Something shifted in them. I saw him looking at me with his defenses totally down. "You want me to take Saint down?"

"I might not make it, like I said. And if I do make it and destroy the defenses in the process, my powers are definitely not going to be what they were beforehand. I might not be strong enough. So I need you to be ready. To do what you have to do."

Daniel wiped his face. It looked like he was rubbing a tear from his eye.

"You're my brother," I said. "Sure, we're not exactly best friends, but we're family. And if there's a chance... Just the smallest chance our sister is still in Saint's hands, then we owe it to each other to find her. Not just that, but we owe it to the world to stop him."

Daniel looked at the waves below. "You've really put the past behind you, haven't you?"

I took a deep breath of the sea air, then I nodded. "I've learned that I can't go hating everyone who's done wrong against me. Sometimes to defeat those you really need to defeat, you need to let go of your own vengeance and focus on forgiveness."

Daniel paused for a second. Then, "Nice speech. So what's the—"

Daniel didn't finish speaking.

A blast of energy smacked into his side.

He went flying toward the sea.

Up above, a group of ULTRAbots dropped their invisibility and watched him fall down to the water.

Their guns were turned on me.

I flew down to Daniel as he fell into the ravenous sea.

Lightning struck above. Torrential rain flew down. The waves grew stronger and stronger. I knew the ULTRAbots weren't far behind me. I could see their bullets blasting past me, firing into the water. Again, that struck me as weird. I was trying to dodge their attacks of course, but my attention was more on stopping Daniel from falling into the sea. He'd taken a bad hit. He was clearly unconscious. I needed him by my side if I was going to carry out my plan of taking down Saint.

But again, why weren't the ULTRAbots' bullets making contact with me? Why weren't they shooting right at me?

I swooped over to the right and picked up my pace toward the water, keen to divert the ULTRAbots' attention from Daniel's falling body. As the water approached, I saw that flashback clearly in my head.

My biological father, Orion, dunking me under the water.

Daniel by one side. My sister, Cassie, at the other side.

The combined abilities of Orion and Saint coming together to make us what we were.

Two generations of the most powerful ULTRAs that ever lived.

I felt the water hit my face and I held my breath. I swam around to where I knew Daniel was going to fall. I had no doubt he could look after himself, but I couldn't bear to lose him. He was unconscious so he was in danger. I couldn't just let him fall.

As I swam around the powerful waves, I got an idea. I knew it was wrong, but it was tempting. Daniel Septer was still Nycto. As much as he was my brother, the rest of the Resistance had a point. When Saint was out of the way, what was stopping him just making another power grab? Did I really need him by my side to take down Saint at all?

Or did I have my golden opportunity to finally get rid of him right here?

I quickly banished that thought from my head when the water splashed.

The ULTRAbots were swimming through the sea, powering toward me.

I moved quicker to where I figured Daniel was about to fall. I'd lost him. He was falling fast, but I'd hit the water quicker than him for a reason. I squinted up as the ULTRAbots got closer. I was putting a lot of attention on holding my breath down here so my powers wouldn't be as...

No. Wait. That wasn't true.

I *would* be as strong.

I'd seen for myself just how strong I could be.

I steadied myself and turned to the ULTRAbots.

I lifted my hands and felt the energy and the power coursing through my system as I looked the ULTRAbots in the eye. They still had that uncertainty to their demeanor, like they were split on what to do, which I still couldn't understand.

Still, I wasn't going to stick around to find out why.

I blasted my hands together and opened up a massive wormhole in the middle of the water. Through it, I could see the desert, somewhere in the Middle East. I watched the ULTRA-bots flood down through that wormhole like they were being flushed down a toilet and felt my energy getting stronger, my powers getting stronger.

I was Kyle Peters. I was Glacies.

I could do this.

I could...

Shit.

Oh shit.

I saw another figure fall down that wormhole and into the desert just as I closed it.

Daniel.

Dammit!

I tried to open up another wormhole in the exact same place, but my powers weren't strong enough. I needed air. I felt like I was getting weaker. Above, I heard more ULTRAbots splash into the water. I could deal with them, sure. But I wasn't totally confident I could hold them off forever.

I tried to open that wormhole again as my oxygen levels dropped and my muscles weakened. In the place of urgency to save Daniel, I felt that vengeance creeping in again. That destructive vengeance which always had a funny way of para-lyzing me.

Saint had done this.

This was Saint's fault.

I was going to make Saint pay for...

No!

I ripped open a wormhole right in front of me. It was the biggest one I'd ever seen, a mass of land and a tunnel of air right in the middle of the water.

It was the desert where Daniel and the ULTRAbots had fallen into.

I let the water carry me out of that wormhole then when I was through, I closed it.

I splashed to the ground below. It must've been the first water this land had seen in a long time. To my left, I saw a man holding a camel with an empty vial of water. He was covered in the seawater, and his jaw was agape.

"This is seawater," I said, holding my hand over it to rip the salt away from as much as I could, purifying it in an instant. "It might still have a salty tang but it should be good for now."

The man didn't say a word back to me. He just looked on, dumbstruck.

I turned ahead to where I'd seen Daniel fall. There was no sign of him.

I thought about going back through that wormhole and dealing with Saint myself. I knew what I was capable of now. I knew how strong I was.

But Daniel was my brother. He'd turned his allegiances to help me. I couldn't just walk away.

I took a deep breath of the scorching desert air and walked through the sand.

I was finding Daniel Septer. I was saving Nycto's life.

If only I'd known then how things were going to turn out.

[38]

An hour searching the desert and still no sign of Daniel Septer.

The air was humid and scorching. As much as I was resistant to the intensity of the weather, even I was struggling to breathe right now. The sand stretched on for miles. There were no sounds here, nothing but total silence. My mouth was dry, my lips chapped. I had no idea where the ULTRAbots had taken Daniel to.

I stopped and put my hands on my knees. I'd been using my powers to fly around this place and try and track Daniel down for a while. But it was useless. There was no sign of him. Plus, using those powers seemed to be taking it out of me more than anything.

I licked my dry lips. I could teleport anywhere and go grab some water, I knew that. But I'd made it this far in my search for Daniel as it was. I wasn't giving up.

A voice in my head asked me why I was doing this. Daniel Septer was still Nycto. He might be my brother, but he'd done some terrible things. He'd hurt Ellicia. He'd threatened my family. Besides, I was strong enough to take Saint down alone.

168 / MATT BLAKE

But another voice—a stronger voice—answered. Yes, Daniel Septer was Nycto, and it didn't matter if he was family or not, he'd still done some terrible things. But then again, Daniel was forced into a harsher upbringing than me. I'd had my sister. I'd had a loving family all around me. Sure, there were a few bullies I had to deal with, but nothing I couldn't handle with the help of my friends.

Daniel didn't have that support around him. He was bullied badly. His family life wasn't great at home, as far as I knew. He had a reason to be angry. Maybe if I'd been in his shoes, I'd have turned out the same way.

The truth was, Daniel was strong. He could help me take down Saint.

And he deserved answers about our sister. I wasn't going to let her fate be a loose end to him.

I was lost in my thoughts when I saw movement in the distance.

I activated my invisibility immediately, then realized if they were ULTRAbots it wouldn't make the blindest bit of difference. I fell to my stomach. Dragged myself forward, right to the top of the sand dune.

Daniel was crouching in the middle of the ULTRAbots. He looked... well. Worryingly relaxed.

The ULTRAbots around him just stood there, not budging.

Weird. It reminded me of the ones that'd tried to fire at me not long ago. They'd shot toward me, but they'd missed. Was something going wrong with them? Or worse—did Saint want us both alive for other reasons?

When I saw the ULTRAbots turn around and lift their guns, I knew I didn't have much more time to speculate.

I ducked their shots. I bolted over to the other side of them with my super-speed, knocking one of their mechanical heads from their shoulders.

I leaped into the air above them and blasted a step of ice into the sky. The ULTRAbots fired at it, distracted by it.

Then I crashed down and stood in the middle of them.

Daniel was on his feet now. His eyes were wide. He looked alarmed.

"Well?" I said, tensing my fists so ice covered them.

Daniel looked at me for a second.

Then he tensed his fists and joined me in the fight back.

I slammed into the chest of an ULTRAbot opposite me. It pushed back with clear strength, dodged my punched, blocked my blasts of ice.

I teleported behind it when it swung at me and wrapped my arm around its neck.

I squeezed tight, feeling the ice creep up my wrist and into my forearm. The ULTRAbot kept on struggling. I saw the ice shifting from my arm to its face, covering it.

Then it elbowed me in the stomach and knocked me back onto the sand.

It walked over to me. Daniel was occupied with ULTRA-bots of his own. It lifted its gun. Held the trigger.

I gritted my teeth.

Clapped my hands.

Above, a wormhole opened up. It lifted the ULTRAbot away, as well as those surrounding Daniel.

They tried to fire back. They tried to struggle free. But they were being lifted away, and there wasn't anything they could do about it.

When they'd disappeared through the wormhole, I clapped my hands and loosened my grip on my powers.

"You okay?" Daniel asked.

"Am I okay? Are *you* okay?"

Daniel raised his hands. "Hey. I'm just asking."

"Well I'm fine. Now I've got you, I'm fine."

"I guess this really does make us even. In a way."

I nodded. "I guess it does."

I stood up and grabbed Daniel's arm.

"What—"

I blasted us away from this desert.

When I opened my eyes, we were back in the middle of the ocean, the torrential rain still lashing down, waves crashing below.

"I think I preferred the desert," Daniel said.

"Yeah, well, beggars can't be choosers."

"What is that?"

"What is what?"

"That saying. I've never heard that before."

"You've never heard 'beggars can't be choosers' before?"

Daniel shook his head.

"You're kidding, right?"

He kept on shaking his head.

I was about to pull him up for not hearing of that phrase before when it dawned on me again why we were here. What I was here to do.

I looked ahead at Saint's tower.

By my side, Daniel looked on, too.

"You ready to do this?" I asked.

Daniel nodded.

I started to move forward. "Wait. Back at the desert. When I found you. What was happening?"

Daniel frowned. "Hmm?"

"You were just... there. And the ULTRAbots weren't doing anything. Why was that?"

Daniel hesitated for a moment. Then he shrugged. "Damned if I know. Now are we getting on with this suicidal plan or what?"

I saw a flicker of Nycto in Daniel's eyes. A look that I didn't like.

It was gone just as soon as I'd seen it.

"It looks like we are," I said.

I took a deep breath and drifted toward Saint's tower.

39

I led the way toward Saint's tower, clueless to how events were going to unfold.

The night sky was jet black. The storm above didn't seem to be letting up, neither did the severity of the waves below. Just up ahead, I saw Saint's tower. It was a remarkable construction when you really took the time to look at it. Jet black, but with a glimmer of jagged silver, much like the edges of his armor. It shot right up into the sky, far above the clouds. He'd built it—with the help of his ULTRAbots—in a matter of days at the very start of his conquest. He didn't have a tower last time during the Era of the ULTRAs. Clearly now he meant business.

There was a humming noise in the air similar to the noise the ULTRAbots made. I figured it was the collective buzz of all the ULTRAbots in there, working away. There was an energy and a life to this place even on the outside. But it was a life that made me feel... unsettled.

I kept my fists gripped tightly in case I had to use my powers fast. There was a smell of burning rubber in the air, so pungent I could taste it. I couldn't wait to be away from here and done with what I had to do. Hopefully, that would be sooner rather than later.

"Watch yourself."

I felt Daniel's hand on my shoulder. He pulled me back.

"We have to be careful when we approach. The second we enter that place, the ULTRAbots will be triggered about our abilities."

I felt that resistance in my mind. The same resistance I'd thrown back at Controlla when he'd stood outside my cell and tried to invade my thoughts. I closed my eyes. "Not if we focus."

I didn't feel anything at first.

Then I felt the push of Saint's tower like it *was* alive.

It was a magnetic feeling, but like two ends pushing against one another. I knew if I let go of my focus, I'd be able to hover in there, but the whole tower would be alerted to my presence. But if I pushed back hard enough... I could break this resistance.

"You're being speculative again," Daniel said.

"Speculation's gonna win us the war."

"You know, I don't like it when you have these lofty ambitions."

"Then go home. I've got work to do."

Daniel didn't go home. Instead, he closed his eyes and joined me in pushing back against the resistance of Saint's tower. We pressed against it, together. I could feel his push too, and I knew that if we focused enough, we could bring this whole thing down and head inside.

And if I failed, Daniel could go on and defeat Saint. I was at ease with that now.

"It's not working," Daniel said.

"Keep focusing."

"What good's focusing when it's not working?"

"Just keep focusing."

Daniel sighed. Then he returned his focus to pushing back against the forces of the tower.

In my head, I saw Saint's mask. I felt myself being submerged under water, my sister beside me. Then I saw myself looking down over her open grave. I'd thought she was dead. Mom and Dad's whole world had been torn apart that day, and Mom would never know the truth about what happened to my sister.

Neither would I. Not completely.

Not if I didn't break through this anti-energy resistance.

I felt the push getting stronger and I knew it was because I was making ground. I gritted my teeth harder. Saw those painful images again, replaying them like a stream stuck on buffering.

"I—I think it's—"

"Ssh," I said.

I dug my nails into my palms and saw Cassie looking back at me in my head. Only she was older. Her hair was long. She was calling out for me, shouting for help.

Behind her, Saint stood smiling.

He dragged her further away from me, and I tasted blood as I bit through my bottom lip.

The push got stronger.

"I can't hold on," Daniel said.

I ignored him and kept on pushing back. My heart pounded so fast I thought it might burst out my chest.

Cassie.

I needed to know the truth about what happened to Cassie.

The only way I'd find the truth was if I came face to face with Saint.

The only way I'd find the truth was if I kept on...

A snap.

I heard a crack in my skull and felt the force back off.

I opened my eyes. Nothing had changed to look at, but the humming noise had weakened.

"Did you hear that?" Daniel asked.

I looked at his surprised face, then back at Saint's tower. "I think we did it."

"Then what are we waiting for?"

We flew into Saint's tower. There was a surprising lack of ULTRAbots around. From memory, this place had been absolutely buzzing with them the last time I'd been here not so long ago.

"It's very quiet," I said.

"It will be at this time," Daniel said, climbing through an opening. "Now come on."

"At this time? What is this time?"

He shrugged. "Changeover time. Come on."

He ran off inside Saint's tower. I wanted to ask him about changeover time and what that meant.

But whatever. I'd have plenty of time to find out when I found Saint.

I followed Daniel down the corridor. It still seemed weird in here. I'd been locked away in one of these many cells lining the tower. I could swear there'd always been more life around than this.

"Something doesn't feel right."

"It's just up here," Daniel said. "We should be able to change the ULTRAbots' focus from here."

He pointed at a door right ahead. My stomach knotted when I imagined what might be behind it. Saint. Saint waiting there for our arrival.

Something seemed off.

But Daniel was right in front of the door, and I knew I couldn't just leave him.

"Wait," I said.

"Come on, bro. All this way and you aren't gonna let me open the door?"

"Just... just wait there. Let me go first. Please."

Daniel shrugged. "Whatever."

I put my hand on the door handle. I thought about tele-porting myself inside, but I didn't know what to expect on the other side.

"Well?" Daniel said. "Waiting for something?"

"If this goes wrong," I said. "You know what you have to do. Right?"

I looked into Daniel's eyes. There was sadness to them just for a second.

Then he half-smiled. "You don't have a thing to worry about."

I nodded. Then I turned back to the door. Held my breath. Lowered the handle.

When I saw what was inside, my body froze.

Ember was standing there. So too was Vortex. Stone. Road-runner. So many other of the Resistance members, all with those bands of anti-energy around their wrists and their bodies, all staring at me.

At the front of the group, Orion.

"What's..."

I went to walk in the room when I saw Saint standing in front of them, hands behind his back.

"Hello, Kyle."

My chest tensed. "Let them—"

I felt a blast of electricity behind me as I tried to use my powers. My hands twisted against my back. I fell to my knees. Every time I tried to use my powers, that electricity shocked me even more.

"Sorry, bro. I mean that. Really."

I saw Daniel Septer walk around me, walk to Saint's side.

I saw them standing together and I knew the truth.

He'd betrayed me. He'd led me and the rest of the Resistance into a trap.

"So," Saint said, his voice deep and echoey. "I think it's about time we had a little chat, don't you?"

40

"So, Kyle. Or Glacies. Or whatever you want me to call you. How does it feel to be on your knees, betrayed by your own brother, and imprisoned with the very 'Resistance' you're supposed to be leading?"

I tried to push back against the bands around my body, but every time I did, a searing bolt of electricity rippled through my system. In front of me in this long, wide room, the Resistance crouched on their knees, all of them with the same bands wrapped around their arms, around their bodies. They looked exhausted, beaten, and bruised. I could tell from the smell of sweat that they'd had a tough battle on their hands too, and most of that battle hadn't been above the streets of New York—it'd been here.

But there was one ULTRA, Saint aside, who didn't have those anti-energy bands around him.

That ULTRA was Daniel Septer. Nycto.

"Traitor," I said. It was about the only word I could gasp out right now.

"Oh don't give Nycto here a hard time," Saint said, patting

Daniel on the back and walking nearer to me. "After all, he was only doing his job."

"You fought beside me. I saved your life."

"And he saved yours, I believe," Saint said, speaking in Daniel's place. Daniel couldn't even look me in the eye anymore. "Brotherly love. It's quite something, isn't it?"

I stared over at Daniel and waited for him to make eye contact with me.

He didn't. Not once.

"Why?" I asked.

Saint smiled. "Of course, I couldn't just send Daniel your way and have him *suddenly* turn to your cause. There needed to be moments of bonding between you. Moments where he saved you and you saved him. There needed to be moments of doubt, too. And I'm absolutely positive you had moments of doubt about Daniel. But in the end, hope prevails. Isn't that just a beautiful thing?"

"You're sick. Both of you. You're sick."

"Not sick," Saint said. "Just... pragmatic. I know what needs to be done to take the world into its next great age, and so too does Daniel."

Saint stretched his hand in my direction and tightened his telekinetic grip around my throat.

"And *you*, my friend, are a very important part of the next stage."

I pushed back against Saint's grip, but that only increased the blast of electricity up my arms and spine even more. I knew I could push against it and fight it, just like I'd proven I could already...

Unless...

Shit. Maybe Saint had lowered the anti-energy shields to this tower all along. Maybe I really wasn't as strong as I thought.

"We needed you here very much," Saint continued. "Of

course, we had to make you *think* we wanted you dead. So there were moments where we put you in absolute peril..."

Being trapped under the falling buildings. The ULTRAbots firing near me, but never totally *at* me, other than the blast through my chest. Was that just a setup too? An illusion by one of Saint's ULTRAs, or even by Daniel? Shit. That'd explain why I'd healed so easily. All of it was making a twisted kind of sense.

"...But all of it was engineered to get you right here. And here you are."

Saint raised his hands. I could feel my anger boiling, bubbling to bursting point.

"My sister," I said. "I know the truth."

Saint laughed. "Oh you know the truth do you? You know the absolute truth?"

"I know you took her. You brought her back."

"You're right about that. But when you say you know the absolute truth, you're wrong. Isn't that right, Orion?"

Saint turned to Orion, who was on his knees. He was gasping. He didn't look in a good way.

"If there's one thing your sister was good at when she got her abilities, it was the power to get into people's heads and make them forget. Brainwash them. She used it against your parents a few times. Made them forget she'd gone out with her friends. Made them forget they were annoyed at her. Just a pity she wasn't around to make your poor grieving family forget she ever existed."

I lunged forward. Electricity shot up my back, paralyzing me.

Saint chuckled. "It's sweet. It really is. A family reunion. That's what we all want, isn't it?"

"What did you do to her?"

Saint's footsteps echoed against the hard floor. "I figured if I had your dear sister, I could hone her abilities. Hone them so she could feed on the abilities of others. And when her abilities were fed, they became stronger."

"What are you talking about?"

Saint crouched down and looked into my eyes. I could see his black eyes behind his mask. "Your sister is very much alive, Glacies. Not only that, but she's the one responsible for the entire brainwashing program so far."

"No," I said.

"Yes. And you'll meet her soon. Only she's... well, she's different now. There's a strong chance she won't remember you. Don't be too alarmed by that. It's nothing personal."

"You're using her. You're using her to—"

"Make the world a better place. Restore some order to humanity. After all, isn't that what we all want, truly? A return of order?"

I shook my head. "You're playing God."

"No. God wants free will for humans. I think free will is the greatest mistake in history. That's what your sister is putting right. But we can only complete that goal if you join her."

I narrowed my eyes. "Me?"

"You see, you're stronger than you think, Kyle. You have abilities hiding under the surface that are just waiting to crash out. Abilities like your sister's. The ability to get into minds. To change things."

"I won't do it. I won't change anyone's mind."

"Oh you will," Saint said. "You won't have much of a choice about that. And when you're connected to your sister's powers, not only will you change minds, but you'll control them. Forever."

A bitter taste filled my mouth when Saint described the future to me. "I won't let that happen."

"You won't have a choice. Anyway." He turned around and

walked in front of the ULTRAs. "All good ULTRAs need lessons teaching. So let's teach you a lesson."

He fired a blast above the room.

A massive wormhole opened up in an instant. Only it wasn't like any I'd ever seen. It was deep black, flickering with electricity. It spiraled around like the head of a tornado. Whatever went in there definitely wasn't coming back.

"How about flame-boy here?" Saint said. He dragged Ember from the ground and held him at the opening of the wormhole. Ember's hair stood on end. Anti-energy crackled across his body as he tried to resist the pull of the wormhole. "Shall we send him to oblivion?"

"No," I said, tears rolling down my cheeks. "Please."

Saint dropped Ember to the ground.

Then he pulled up Vortex by her ankle.

"How about this one?" he asked.

I lunged forward, then fell again. I tried to fight against the electricity, but it was no use. I was trapped.

"Ooh, you like this one. I'd be jealous if I were you, flame-boy. Seems like he cares about the girl more than he cares about you."

"Stop this!"

When I shouted out, I looked into Daniel's eyes. They were bloodshot. He didn't look like he was enjoying this as much as Saint. If anything, he looked uncertain.

But he wasn't doing anything to stop what was occurring.

Saint dropped Vortex back down. "Okay, okay. The girl's safe. The girl gets away with it. You care about her, but not enough. We need someone else. Someone you really care about. Who could that be?"

My stomach tensed and my body froze when I realized who Saint was referring to.

He lifted Orion.

Orion didn't fight. He just let Saint lift him.

"Please!" I lunged forward again and shook with every blast of electricity. Although I knew it could kill me, I didn't care. I couldn't let Saint throw Orion into that wormhole. I couldn't watch my real dad die.

"Yeah," Saint said, as he lifted Orion higher. "I think this is the one."

"Orion!"

Saint smiled as he held Orion right in front of the wormhole. Orion stared down at me. There wasn't any emotion on his face. Just a cold look.

"I guess it's always been about you and me really, hasn't it, old boy?" Saint said. "Well now it's time to settle the score. Now it's time to put you somewhere you won't come back from, just like you did me. Only you really, really won't come back from this place."

"Orion, please!"

I knew my voice was falling on deaf ears. I looked at Daniel. His eyes were even more bloodshot. He was shaking.

"He's our dad, Daniel," I whimpered. "Orion's our dad. Don't let this happen. Please."

Daniel met my eyes for the first time since he'd betrayed me.

Then he looked around at Orion as he got within inches of the wormhole.

"Never mind," Saint said. "Too late."

He threw Orion into the wormhole, clapped his hands and closed it.

I screamed out. I kicked. I did everything I could to break free of my ties.

But as the electricity burned my body, all I could see in my mind was Orion's hard face as he looked back down at me.

Then, the moment he disappeared.

Forever.

41

I sat in the same cell I'd been thrown into with the rest of the Resistance some time ago and I didn't even try to break out. Not this time.

I didn't know what time of day it was, or what the weather was like outside. Damn, it could be any time of *year* for all I knew. I'd been locked away in this cell without leaving for what felt like forever now. I was cold. Tired. My head ached, and the taste of vomit constantly stung my lips. Outside, I heard the rattling and buzzing of the ULTRAbots back at work. There were plenty of them around now, which further convinced me that Nycto had lured me here with the intention of trapping me all along.

My back ached from the electricity that had stung up it so many times. The anti-energy bands around had a way of affecting me like that. I'd tried to fight them in the early days and break free. But I saw now that fighting was pointless. These bands were stronger than the first batch. There was no way I was getting through them. I was stuck here. Everything was lost. There wasn't a thing left to fight for. I just had to wait for the moment that the end finally arrived.

I didn't know when it would arrive. Just that it would, soon enough.

The sensation of that electricity had a doubly bad effect because of what it reminded me of. I saw that wormhole opening up above the room Saint had ambushed me in, after Nycto slapped the bands onto me and brought me to my knees. I saw Saint lifting Ember up to the wormhole, then dropping him. I saw him lifting Vortex up there, then dropping her too.

And then I saw him lifting Orion.

Sickness crippled my stomach every time I thought of that moment, and of the way Orion had looked down at me. It wouldn't have been quite as bad if he'd said something. Just anything. The man was my dad. I needed him to tell me everything was going to be okay.

He hadn't. Instead, he'd just looked at me and said nothing like he was waiting for me to figure it out for myself.

"What do you want?" I muttered to myself. I tightened my fists and banged against the solid metal floor. "What do you want?"

Of course, nobody answered. The ULTRAbots ignored me, as they always did. I was alone here. I had no idea where the rest of the Resistance were at. Wherever they were, I knew for a fact they wouldn't be winning. Saint's brainwashing program was well underway. The ULTRAbot armies were growing.

I was the final piece in that brainwashing puzzle and I knew my time was approaching. Fast.

"What do you want from me?" I whispered.

I remembered Orion, then. I remembered what he'd told me about forgiveness being a far stronger force than vengeance. How could he be telling the truth when he said that? After all, I'd forgiven Nycto. I'd seen him as Daniel Septer, my brother, and how had that worked out for me? He'd betrayed me. He'd lured me here after elevating my trust and he'd watched as

Orion was thrown into a wormhole he wasn't ever coming back from.

I thought about Orion floating around that wormhole in the middle of nowhere and I wondered if he still believed that forgiveness was stronger than vengeance.

But then I remembered something else. The looks Daniel and I had shared since his identity had been revealed. I didn't want to believe they were all fake. I *couldn't* believe they were all fake.

And if they weren't all fake, then what did it mean?

I tensed my fists when the realization dawned on me.

Saint wanted to use me to help aid my sister's abilities to control the brainwashed humans. He claimed I was the final piece of the puzzle.

But what if I wasn't?

I tried to tense my fists but felt that electricity right away. I kept on pressing though, holding my ground. I remembered what Saint told me. My sister had the ability to get inside people's minds and change their direction, and so did I. He'd said it himself, and he had no idea what he'd done when he had.

He'd made me realize I wasn't crazy. I could get into the minds of other people, other ULTRAs.

Which meant I could deflect their powers just as I'd deflected Controlla's.

I pushed harder against the electricity. If I could resist the mind control, then I could resist anything. I had to make it work. It was all I had left.

I wasn't going to let my sister be subject to a life of control like this. I owed it to Mom. To Dad. To Orion. To everyone.

I even owed it to Daniel.

I tightened my fists and closed my eyes as the electricity freely flowed through my body.

For a second, just a split second, I felt a speck of ice freeze on my palms.

"Well, well," a voice said, snapping me from my trance. I fell down, the electricity stopping.

Saint was right outside my cell. Behind him, four ULTRAbots.

In front of them, there was a metallic bed on wheels.

"It's time for the final stage of your family reunion," Saint said. "And then we'll get on with the beginning of the next era."

The cell door opened.

I knew there was no escape now.

But I felt that little speck of ice on my palms melting away and I wondered...

42

Earlier...

Daniel Septer couldn't help feeling guilty for what he'd done.

He sat in Saint's office and looked out at the vast ocean. The storm was settling. The rain wasn't falling as heavily anymore, and the waves had eased. The sun was rising. If he distanced himself from his thoughts enough, he could convince himself he was back home, in his bedroom, playing video games, the source of enjoyment in his past life.

But every time he got close to convincing himself he was back there in an ordinary world, he felt the weight of his powers in his hands and he remembered what he'd done.

"You did well, Nycto."

Saint's voice boomed out from behind him. He didn't turn around and look at Saint. He didn't want Saint to see any trace of disappointment in his eyes.

He felt a hand on his shoulder and it made his muscles tense.

"I understand it must've been difficult watching what

happened earlier," Saint said. There was a rare understanding to his words.

"I understand."

"I know it can't have been easy. Watching your father disappear into that wormhole. But you know it was for the greater good. You see that, don't you?"

The difficult part about all this? Daniel wasn't sure he did see that anymore. He thought Saint's plan was genius when he'd first heard it. Bond with his biological brother, then take everything away from him. Kyle was the missing piece of the jigsaw puzzle that Saint needed to conquer humanity. The other half of the puzzle? His sister. It was a lot to take in, and it was finally catching up with him.

Saint took his hand from Daniel's shoulder, breaking him from his train of thoughts. "Of course you see. You're Nycto. The most powerful ULTRA in existence, myself aside. And one day, when my time is up, all of this will be yours."

He held his arms out. Daniel looked around at the metallic room. He heard the hum of the ULTRAbots inside the tower. Outside, he saw the sun reflecting against the ocean.

He wanted all this. That had been his plan. But now he was being offered it and really seeing the consequences, Daniel just wasn't sure. He thought he'd hated Kyle Peters, Glacies. He thought he hated the whole Resistance and what it stood for. But that was before he *saw* what the other side was like.

ULTRAs fighting for one another. Inclusion. Respect.

He'd earned it. And then he'd gone and thrown it all away for what? A world that he might rule one day.

"Anyway. Before we start the final process, I'm sure you'll want to meet her, won't you?"

"Meet who?"

Saint smiled. "Your sister."

A bitter taste covered Daniel's lips. He looked away. "I... I guess I—"

"She doesn't remember a thing about the world before. That's unfortunate, I suppose. But it's still only right that you meet her. It might just make you feel better. You'll see you're doing the right thing after all."

The idea of meeting a sister Daniel didn't even know existed up until recently was bizarre, but he couldn't deny that he was curious. "She won't know a thing?"

"She can barely speak. Her mind is too focused on control. She's been satiating her hunger. Feeding on the powers of the ULTRAs. Soon she won't need any more food. She'll just need her brother beside her."

Daniel looked at the floor. The thought of Kyle being hooked up to Saint's plan didn't sit right with him, not anymore.

But then what other choice did he have?

"I'll meet her. On one condition."

Saint held his stare. "And what would that be?"

Daniel took a deep breath. He couldn't believe he was actually going ahead with these words. "Stone. Ember. Vortex. Roadrunner. Let them live."

Saint's stare didn't break. "What?"

"They might've been part of the Resistance but I met them. I spoke with them. They can see our side of things, I know they can."

"And what makes you so certain?"

"I just... I just know. Please."

Daniel felt the anger in the room building. He could feel Saint's fury, tangible and infectious. He waited for Saint to tell him he was in the wrong, and there was no chance he would let the ULTRAs he'd mentioned off the hook.

"You don't need to worry about those four," Saint said. "I let them go. We don't need them anymore. They are free to fight, for now. But their fight will be futile once Kyle and his sister's powers combine. Now come on. Let's go see your sister."

Saint walked out of his office and toward the corridors of his tower. Daniel took a deep breath of the clammy air and followed Saint out of his office. The pair of them descended right to the bottom of the tower. They walked into the room where masses of unconscious humans lay, ready for conversion. Then they went into a smaller, dark corridor on the left of the room.

At the end of the corridor, there was a glass window.

Bright light shone from behind it.

"Go on," Saint said. "She's in there."

Daniel looked at Saint, his hands sweaty. Then he looked back at the bright light.

He didn't want to face her. He was afraid of what he might see.

But he walked anyway.

As he got closer to the window, he became aware of a presence in that room. And then he saw her.

She had long blonde hair. She must've been in her late teens or early twenties, but her face looked younger, like it'd been preserved. Her eyes were wide open, but there was no life in them.

Just a beam of blue light.

As he looked at her lying there, his sister, Daniel wanted nothing more than to go in there and break her out, get them both away from here.

Then he felt a blast of electricity hit his back.

He fell down and struggled on the floor, completely paralyzed. When he managed to find the strength to roll over, he looked up and saw Saint staring down at him, electricity in his hands.

"Stupid, naive little boy," Saint said.

"What—"

192 / MATT BLAKE

Another blast of electricity crackled across Daniel's body, totally restraining his powers.

"I told you Kyle Peters was the missing piece of the jigsaw. And that's true. But there's another piece, too. And if you hadn't been so dumbly blinded by power, you might've seen what that missing piece was sooner."

As Saint lifted his hands to blast another bolt of electricity into him, Daniel realized with a sinking stomach exactly what he was talking about.

"You played me," he said. "All this time, you... you played me."

"And now the games are over," Saint said. "It's time to get you strapped down and hooked up. I've got a planet to conquer."

The electricity hit Daniel again and this time, he passed out.

43

I couldn't do a thing as Saint's ULTRAbots pushed me along to the room where my entire world would end—and *the* entire world as I knew it would end.

I was strapped down to a metal bed on wheels. Those anti-energy ties were wrapped around my arms and my legs. There were so many of them that I only had to twitch my powers to trigger them.

Up above, I saw the masses of ULTRAbots swirling around. They didn't even look down at me, unaware of what was about to occur. And it struck me that this was the fantasy Saint wanted. He wanted a cold, lifeless existence. He wanted people and ULTRAbots to obey him rather than have minds of their own. He was so insecure about his ability to lead that he had to find ways to cheat leadership. That's what he really was.

Just a pity he was the most powerful thing in existence right now.

I heard the footsteps behind me, pushing me along. My mouth tasted of blood from the many times I'd tried to use my powers while trapped away in that cell. I'd used them so much that I'd thought about giving up.

But not now. I was going to fight, if it was the last thing I did.

I knew where I was going. These ULTRAbots were taking me to my sister. It still seemed weird, accepting this fact. My sister was alive. All this time, she was alive, and she had abilities too. Only Saint was manipulating those abilities for his own benefit.

Soon, he'd be manipulating my abilities for his own benefit.

Unless I found a way to fight.

I felt myself lowering down toward where Daniel—or Nycto, as I now referred to him again after his cowardly betrayal —took me when I was first locked away in these cells. My stomach tightened, and my powers bubbled close to the surface. All this time and I'd been so close to my sister. So close, without realizing.

I hoped I wasn't too late to save her. I hoped there was something I could do.

The door in front of me opened. I tilted my head forward. There were even more humans lying across those beds now. Some of them, right at the far end, were hobbling off the beds, those who'd been brainwashed and turned. A few of them immediately saw to their duties, getting down on their knees and scrubbing the floor. It horrified me that this industrial hell was heaven for Saint. This was everything he'd been working to.

The bed took a sharp turn and the next thing I knew I was being pushed through into a dark corridor. I couldn't see what was in that corridor, only that there was a bright blue light at the end of it through a wide window.

It didn't take a genius to see this was my destination. I knew it. I could just *feel* it.

The ULTRAbots stopped walking me when we reached the window. They walked away from my side, leaving me alone in the dark. At first, I thought they'd be right back. But when they didn't return, I started to get agitated. I knew there was someone behind that glass, but they were just out of sight. I had to see them. I had to look them in the eye and—

A shock of electricity right down my spine.

I fell back against the bed as the anti-energy bands fried my body. I took some deep breaths, regathered my composure. I couldn't be rash. I had to think ahead. I couldn't make any crazy decisions.

I heard a door slide open. Then, footsteps echoed closer to me. I didn't have to look at whoever was walking to know that it was Saint.

I heard the footsteps stop right behind me. Then, silence again. Total stillness.

It was only minutes later after much more agitation and another blast of electricity that Saint finally spoke.

"It's time," he said.

He grabbed the back of my metal bed and wheeled me around. I pushed back as we headed toward the door into the light room. I felt like a kid on a rollercoaster, only one that I was hating and was eager to get off.

"Take a few deep breaths, Glacies," Saint said. "They'll be the last you remember."

He pushed me through into the light. It was so bright that it blinded my eyes.

When my eyes adjusted, I saw her.

Her blonde hair was just as thick and lush as I remembered. She didn't look much older at all, and I guessed that must be something to do with the weird not-quite-living, not-quite-dead state she'd survived in all these years.

I felt a tear roll down my face. My throat bobbed.

There was no doubt. There was absolutely no doubt.

The girl across the room, tied down to a bed like me, was Cassie.

Saint pushed me up beside her. I saw then that she was covered in wires. There was a light to her eyes. I knew what they must be. The brain signals that were being sent out to the masses. Soon, I'd be just like her.

Unless I could do something about it.

"Cassie," I said.

She didn't do anything. She didn't even acknowledge my voice.

More tears rolled down my face. "Cassie. Please. Just… just hear me."

I realized then that I'd have to do something that'd cause me a lot of pain.

I embraced all my anger, all my love, and filled my body with powers.

I felt electricity shock me all over. Every urge in my body told me to stop because I was doing myself damage. But I couldn't.

Please, Cassie. Wake up.

I kept on trying to reach out for her as the anti-energy currents got stronger. I could feel her powers, tangible in the air. If I could just break through them and get through to her, just as I had with Controlla's, then I could wake her up. We could get out of here. Together.

But the anti-energy got stronger.

My body convoluted harder.

Please, Cassie! It's Kyle. Please!

My body went weak, then. I saw smoke rising up from my chest, smelled it in the air. I was broken. Completely broken. All my strength was gone.

Saint stepped over me. He lifted the needle by his side, the one that was attached to Cassie's body at one side and an ancient looking machine at the other. "Don't fight anymore. You're going to need all your strength for what's next."

I ignored him and pushed back against the anti-energy once again. I felt myself getting closer to my sister, inching further into her mind, invading her thoughts and ending all of this.

"Rest, my child. Rest."

I felt the needle stick into my arm and my muscles started to go weak. When I tried to use my powers, my arms just spasmed. My powers were weakening. They were being taken away.

I kept on fighting, kept on trying to reach out to my sister, as my body got weaker, as my vision distorted. And as I faded away, I felt okay again. I felt like I was back at home, in the first eight years of my life, Cassie by my side.

I felt normal again.

I felt like I didn't have to fight anymore.

"Good," Saint said. "Very good. One more sibling and we're ready..."

I didn't properly hear Saint's final words.

I took a deep breath of the cool air.

Then I let that breath go.

My eyes closed, and I drifted off into a comfortable, warm sleep...

44

Stone held his ground as another mass of ULTRAbots emerged over the top of Los Angeles.

It was barely light but already the day was warm. By his side, Roadrunner, Ember, Vortex and the rest of the Resistance. When he said the rest of the Resistance, there wasn't very damned many. Thirty, maybe forty at a push.

But Saint had let them go 'cause he thought they weren't strong enough to take him down, and because he said he didn't need him for that weird program of his anymore. That he had a better plan in place.

Well he was damned dumb for feeling that way. 'Cause the Resistance were gonna fight to the end, especially after what Saint did to Orion.

"This isn't gonna be easy, folks," Stone shouted, as the number of ULTRAbots thickened. "But the truth is, there's people here. And where there's people, they need protecting."

Vortex nodded. So too did Ember.

They'd heard mixed things about how effective rescuing people from LA really was. Apparently, it wasn't that big a deal anyway. There'd be a way to get them without needing to physically have the people nearby to brainwash soon. The whole reason Saint had taken a group of humans up to his tower was just for the first phase of brainwashing.

The second phase was so, so close.

But Stone and the Resistance would be damned if they let anything happen to the people of this city.

"How long do you think we can hold 'em off?" Ember asked.

Stone swallowed a lump in his throat. The ULTRAbot cloud grew greater. "As long as it..."

He saw something then. A ball of light right under the ULTRAbots. It started small, but it was growing rapidly by the second.

"What in God's name is that?" Vortex asked.

Stone didn't know for definite what that ball of light was. "I can take a damned good guess."

He didn't have to say anything else 'cause he knew the Resistance would suspect the same thing. It was the ball of energy that was going to brainwash this city and every other city across the world. Sure, defending the people of LA wasn't gonna defend everyone on the planet.

But it was a start.

"What do we do about a ball of light like that?" Vortex asked.

Stone took a deep breath of the thick morning air. "We do what we do best," he said. "We show 'em how tough we are."

He tensed his fists and felt rock cover his body.

Beside him, Vortex's eyes rolled back into her skull.

Beside her, Ember's hands erupted in flames.

Beside him, Roadrunner's legs started spinning in midair.

And behind the four of them, the rest of the Resistance activated their powers.

"Now," Stone shouted.

He flew up toward the ULTRAbots. Almost right on cue, the ULTRAbots flew back at him.

He smashed the first one across the jaw, splitting it in two upon contact. He kicked the next one in the chest, sending it right into the middle of that ball of energy. On the ground below, he watched as some of the citizens of LA made their way out of town, sneaking as far away as they could. Stone wasn't sure about that. He preferred that everyone just stayed put so he knew the whereabouts of everyone he was fighting for.

But he had to focus on the goddamned task at hand right now.

He had to hold off the ULTRAbots, and he had to protect these people.

That's what Orion would've wanted.

That's what Glacies would've wanted.

He slammed into more of them. They fired back, and he took the bulk of their fire, shielding Vortex and the rest of the team. Roadrunner skipped around the ULTRAbots, confusing them with her speed and making them shoot one another. Vortex puzzled them even more, and Ember fired a flamethrower from either hand, incinerating both the ULTRA-bots themselves and their bullets.

"Keep pushing back!" Stone cried.

He'd never considered himself a leader. Even when he was sent to correctional for bad behavior as a kid, he'd been one of the quiet ones. He'd always been pretty surprised by his own strength, in truth. It'd made him feel shy. Right from when he was young, he'd had biceps bigger than tree trunks. He kept them covered up because he felt like he'd cheated them in some way. He never exercised, never stayed fit. They just kinda... well, happened.

It was only when he got pissed at his parents for grounding

him one night and stones sprouted across his body that he knew he was really, truly different.

The ULTRAbots pushed back harder. More bullets fired into him. He couldn't stop all of them, and many of them blasted past him, heading toward the ground below.

"There's too many of 'em!" Ember called.

Stone shook his head and plucked another ULTRAbot from the sky, then threw it back at the rest of its crew. "No."

"It's not a yes or a no, Stone," Ember said. "There's too goddamned many of them."

Stone looked at the mass of ULTRAbots. The sky was absolutely covered in them. He didn't want to accept defeat. He wanted to believe the Resistance could go on long after Orion and Glacies were gone.

But right now it didn't seem like they were strong enough. Right now, it felt like they were pegged down.

He looked down at the ground. In the distance, he knew the Diablo Canyon Power Plant, a nuclear electricity-generating station, was sitting there, untouched. He'd had a thought for a while now. He just wasn't sure he could go through with it.

Now, he saw he had to.

"Keep on holding them off," Stone shouted. "And make sure the people of this city get far, far away."

Vortex narrowed her eyes. "What?"

"Just keep on fighting."

"But where are you—"

"I won't be long. There's somethin' I have to do."

Stone shot through the sky and away from LA before anyone had a chance to protest. He looked over at the nuclear plant as he approached. Saw the tall structures still rumbling away.

He knew what he had to do.

He felt all the anger and all the pain that'd been building up his entire life.

He crashed down in the grounds of the plant.

Then he beat his way underneath the nuclear plant. He ripped it out of the ground, the whole damned thing. The lift was hard. He bit down onto his rocky lips as the stone covered places it'd never covered before. He was convinced this plant was going to crush him.

But then he stood there with it above his head, the whole thing balanced over him.

He flew into the sky again then. Holding the nuclear plant on his back was tough; nigh on impossible. His flight was slower for it. He was constantly fearful of plummeting down toward the ground.

But he kept on pushing. He kept on going. 'Cause he owed it to the Resistance. He owed it to humanity.

After more torturous pushing, he saw the cloud of ULTRA-bots up ahead.

They were still fighting. They were getting closer to the city. Ember, Vortex, and Roadrunner were struggling, and so were the rest of the Resistance, more of them falling.

"Ember!" Stone shouted. The shout was louder than any he'd ever let out. It boomed across the land, echoed through the buildings.

Ember looked around at Stone.

So too did all the ULTRAbots.

"Do it," Stone screamed, tears building in his eyes. "When I get to the middle of them, do it."

Stone didn't wait to find out whether Ember agreed.

He just flew at the ULTRAbots.

He took the fire of all their bullets, blocking the nuclear plant from the ULTRAbot attack as well as he could.

He flew faster as the Resistance distracted the ULTRAbots some more, as he hurtled toward the heart of this brainless army.

When he was inches away, his body hardly able to hold on anymore, pieces of rock falling down from him, he saw his mom and dad in his mind. He saw his brother, Stuey. He pictured them up in the Canadian mountains on a trek, so happy, so together. He wanted to be with them again.

"Maybe one day," he said, tears rolling down his face. "Maybe one damned day."

He flew to the middle of the ULTRAbots.

"Now!" he screamed.

The ULTRAbots all held their guns but didn't fire, clearly fully aware of what he was holding, of what it meant.

"I—I can't," Ember shouted.

"Do it. Goddamned do it. Now!"

Stone closed his eyes.

He didn't watch to see if Ember did it.

But when he felt the blast and heard it fill his ears, he knew. He knew damned well he'd done what he had to do.

His last thought was of Orion disappearing into that wormhole, and of Glacies fighting away for the good of humanity. The many times he'd fought to save Stone's life.

Well there was no saving his life this time. He knew that now.

And he was protecting the Resistance—he was helping humanity—so he was totally cool with that.

The blast cracked his rocky body into pieces.

Light seared through his closed eyes.

He bit down onto his stony lips and pictured everyone good in his life.

Then, he saw nothing.

45

I felt myself slipping further and further into nothingness.

There was a bright blue light ahead of me. It felt warm. I wanted to go to it, but something in my body told me I shouldn't because it was bad for me. I didn't know why. I didn't know where I was, what I was doing, or even *who* I was.

All I wanted to do was go toward that blue light.

As I drifted closer to it, total relaxation covering my fluid body, I realized there was a girl standing behind that blue light. Something told me I recognized her. That she was familiar. I wasn't sure when from, but it made me want to go to that light even more.

When I got even closer, it dawned on me who the girl was. It was my sister, Cassie. I'd thought she was dead, but here she was, wherever *this* was, alive.

I had to go to her. I had to reach her. I'd failed to reach her when I was younger, in the middle of the Great Blast. I wasn't going to fail again.

But still something tugged at my back and told me to stop moving because moving toward her was bad news.

The counter-voice soon faded though, drifting away like

consciousness in a lucid dream. I felt that warm blue light covering my body. I felt it slipping through my skin, through my muscles, right through to my bones. I drifted so close to my sister's side that she was right beside me.

She looked at me with those bright blue eyes. It didn't look like she recognized me.

"Cassie," I said, my voice distorted and soft. "It's me. It's..."

It hit me then. Made my stomach knot in an instant. I remembered who I was, what I was doing here. I remembered exactly what was happening.

Cassie and I had been connected.

Saint was trying to use us to brainwash every last human left on the planet, and keep them that way.

And had he said something about *another* sibling being involved too?

I pushed back against the draw of the light, but when I did that, my body singed with electricity.

"Cassie," I said, my heart racing. "We—we can't do this. You have to wake up."

She didn't seem to hear me. She just looked at me like she could only slightly make out a voice.

"It's Kyle. It's your brother. It's... it's me, Cassie."

Every time I pushed against the draw of that blue light, I felt the resistance getting stronger. I knew what it was. It was similar to the anti-energy that stung me whenever I tried to fight against those bands.

But I'd fought through those bands before, just like I'd fought through the powers of Controlla.

I could reverse that resistance. I could use it in my favor.

"Cassie," I said. I could see the blue light getting stronger and I wanted so badly to move toward it. "You need to hear me. It's Kyle. Saint's got you. He wants you to brainwash everyone on this planet. You can't let him do that. You have to fight."

The blue light got stronger. The pain in my body intensified.

"Cassie!" I said, tears rolling. "See what you're doing. See what this is. Please. It's me, sis. It's me."

Just for a split second, I saw the blue light in Cassie's eyes fade. I saw her look at me and recognize me.

"Kyle?" she said.

Just as she said my name, my fight against the resistance slipped.

The blue light returned to her eyes.

It dragged me in toward it, and I slipped away.

It covered my body, and I felt it surround me.

Then I felt it pour out of my own eyes.

Then I felt nothing but pure power.

Pure control.

46

Miriam Carter stared into the sky at the growing ball of light.

It was only morning, but it was boiling hot as that ball of light grew. Miriam was just outside West Hollywood. Her two children, Paddy and Michael, were beside her.

"What's happening, Mommy?"

Miriam tried to be as reassuring as she could to the kids. But it wasn't easy, especially when she could see the truth right in front of her. "You two don't worry. Everything's gonna be okay."

"Are the ULTRAs still fighting the bad ones away?"

A bitter taste filled Miriam's mouth. She'd watched the ULTRAs fight back against the ULTRAbots. She'd watched as one of them flew back with something massive above him— something she recognized in her final moments as a nuclear power plant.

She'd watched as it exploded, taking the army of ULTRA-bots with it.

Only that explosion had been swallowed up by the ball of light.

And the ball of light just kept getting bigger.

"Mommy?" Michael asked. "Are they?"

"Yes," Miriam said. She closed the curtains and walked over to her kids. "Now you come here and give your mommy a hug, okay?"

"Eww," Paddy said, acting older than his years.

"Don't you 'eww' me. You're never too old to give your mommy a hug."

She held her children tight and felt a lump in her throat as the ball of light grew bigger outside. She knew what'd happen when it engulfed her and her children. She'd heard the rumors of brainwashing. She didn't want to accept that it was going to happen to her, but she couldn't see any other way now.

It was happening. All she could do was hold her children so they didn't feel afraid.

"I love you boys," Miriam said, as the humming noise from the light inched above the house. "You know that, don't you?"

"I love you too, Mommy," Michael said.

Paddy hesitated. Then, he spoke too. "And me."

Miriam felt a warm tear drip down her cheek as she held her boys tightly.

The light beamed in through the windows.

Her memory started to blur.

She knew her time was almost up.

She held her breath, held her kids and prayed for a miracle...

47

I felt the blue light fill my body and I knew there was no turning back now.

In the distance, through my mind's eyes, I saw cities and towns. Some of them were empty, but others were still filled with people. I felt a huge ball of energy growing in front of me. I knew what it was. It was the light that was going to brainwash the last remaining humans. It was the mass of energy that my sister and I had created by Saint linking our powers.

I wanted to stop it. I wanted to fight it.

But I knew I couldn't do a thing about it.

I looked to my right and saw Cassie staring out at this sphere of energy in front of us. Her neck was back, and blue light, like electricity, flowed from her eyes and mouth. I wanted to try and reach out to her and beg her to stop this, because I knew that if we could cause this kind of negative energy together, then we could turn it into a strong, positive energy too.

But I couldn't do a thing about it.

I felt the light burn through the tips of my fingers, and burst out of my paralyzed body.

I couldn't help crying about all this. Here I was, beside the sister who I'd been convinced was dead for eight years. Mom and Dad had believed she was dead too. Mom had died thinking she was dead. Our reunion should've been a happy thing. A positive thing.

But it wasn't. It wasn't even a reunion at all.

I thought of that split second Cassie had looked into my eyes and recognized me. We'd both clicked and acknowledged who each other were, before being dragged back in by the might of our own powers.

She'd looked at me. She'd known who I was.

So no matter how hard it was, I could make her see the truth. If I fought as hard as I could, I could bring Cassie back from this. I could bring the pair of us back from this.

I wondered if she was experiencing thoughts like I was, too. Maybe she was, and she also thought it was too difficult to fight against these powers building inside us.

"No," I said, the words nigh-on-impossible to speak. "We... can... fight."

I held my breath and pushed against the paralysis my body was in. I tried to stretch every muscle, tried to cry out and scream because I just had to break free and Cassie had to break free.

We couldn't let the world beneath us fall. We couldn't watch it crumble.

I saw images flash into my mind as my body vibrated. The convulsions were violent and hard. If I shook any harder, I knew I could do some damage.

Screw it. So what if I did some damage? So what if I killed myself trying to get out of this?

I was doing whatever I could to get my sister and I out of this mess, even if it ended my life.

I gritted my teeth together, hard. My life flashed before my eyes. Painful memories. Memories of being dunked under that water with Cassie and Daniel either side of me. Memories of growing up, being bullied, having my lunch money stolen.

But most of the memories started to turn into good memories. I thought of the people I loved. Mom. Dad. Damon. Avi. Ellicia. All those people who'd made my life something positive for all these years. I was doing this for them. Not just for me, not just for my sister, but for them.

The resistance pushed back at me harder. In front, I could see a massive ball of light now. It looked as big as the earth itself. I knew if I let it grow any larger, it'd just swallow the planet whole, and the world would never be the same again. Ever.

The world would be Saint's.

"I'm not letting that happen!" I shouted.

Shouting was agony. My lungs felt like they were being squeezed between vice grips. But I resisted the urge to give up fighting and focused my attention on Cassie. I was weak. I didn't have much left.

But what I did have left, I was going to use to get her back.

"Cass-ie," I gasped.

She didn't respond. The ball of energy grew larger.

"Cassie. It's... It's Kyle. It's—"

A searing pain lurched through my body. I felt it in every single muscle from head to toe like hot needles were being wedged through me.

And still I kept on fighting.

"Cassie we need to—to stop this. It's me. It's your brother. And you—you need to fight. Even though it's painful you need to fight."

I felt like my words were falling on deaf ears. But that didn't matter. At least I was trying. At least I was fighting.

I twisted my neck around, a maneuver that made my spine feel like it split. "Look at me, Cassie. Just... just fight the pain and look at me."

212 / MATT BLAKE

Cassie kept on staring ahead. Energy moved through her body, out of her eyes.

"Look at me, Cassie!"

Still, she looked onwards.

I felt tears fall down my face then. I knew what this meant. I'd pushed everything I had. I'd done everything I could. One more exertion and I was pretty certain it was game over for me.

I felt the resistance pushing back at me, just egging me on to continue and break myself.

"Screw it," I said, my voice weak and crackly. "Screw it."

I closed my eyes and let every inch of power leave my body.

In my mind, as that power left, I heard myself saying Cassie's name. I heard myself screaming it, and then reaching out and trying to drag her out of her paralysis.

My body was on fire.

Everything was agony.

But still I pressed. I pushed through the wall of energy fighting back at me. I felt my power's arms wrapping around Cassie, whispering in her ear, telling her who I was and that everything was going to be okay.

Then, with the last of my strength, I saw Ellicia in my mind, and more tears rolled down my face.

"I love you," I said.

Then I dragged Cassie out of her cocoon of energy.

I heard an explosion. It ripped through this weird non-body reality. Then I opened my eyes and saw I was back on that bed. Electricity was sparking around me. The ULTRAbots who'd put me on this bed and hooked me up were all on the floor, smoke rising from their bodies.

Saint lay flat on the floor, too.

I lifted myself forward, my hands shaking. The anti-energy bands had come loose. Power tingled at the surface.

I'd done it.

I'd broken out.

I'd—

"Kyle?"

When I heard her voice, even though eight years had passed, it was just as I'd remembered.

I turned around.

Cassie was sitting on the edge of her bed. Her eyes were wide. She looked confused. Terrified.

But she was looking right at me.

"Kyle?" she said. "Is... is that really you?"

I went to open my mouth but my jaw shook.

I went to speak, but instead I cried.

I went to grab her hand to get us out of here, but instead I just ran over her and fell into her arms.

I made the contact with her I'd been waiting to make ever since I ran toward her eight years ago and watched her fall.

"Sis," I said, crying. "I've missed you. I've missed you."

"You too, little brother. You too."

We both held on to each other.

We didn't want to let go. Not again.

We just stood there and held each other and cried.

Miriam held her arms around her boys as the massive ball of energy approached.

She saw the light surround her even though her eyes were squeezed tightly shut. Warm tears streamed down her cheeks, which she could taste on her lips. She smelled the hair of her two boys and imagined she was cuddling them in their beds after lulling them to sleep with a bedtime story. What she'd do to be back home again. What she'd do for everything to be back to normal again.

She felt her hair stand on end. A force pulled against her, and she knew what it meant. Her memories would soon be gone. Her consciousness would soon be gone. Everything she knew and loved would disappear around her in an instant.

"I love you," she whispered. She wasn't sure if her children heard her, because a deafening static sound blasted out of this ball of energy, reminding her just how powerful it actually was. "Boys, I love you."

She held them tighter.

Michael's arms clung around her.

Paddy tucked his head closer under Miriam's neck.

And then there was a loud pop, and nothing.

Miriam kept her eyes closed after she heard the bursting noise. She was convinced that was it. Everything was over.

But she was still having these rational thoughts. So there had to be something, right?

She opened her eyes.

The light had gone. The ball of energy had disappeared.

Michael and Paddy were still in her arms.

She looked at them just to check they were okay, that their minds were still present.

"Boys? Are you okay? Boys?"

They looked up at Miriam with a deathly stare.

Then, "Are we okay now?"

Miriam lunged down to her boys and squeezed them again. They stood there, hugging each other, crying together, like so many families across the world.

"Thank you, God," she said. "Thank you."

She'd prayed for a miracle.

She'd got a miracle.

Her boys were still here.

And she was still here for them.

[49]

I wanted to hold on to Cassie forever, but I had more urgent matters at hand.

Like getting out of Saint's tower and destroying it. For good.

I pulled back from Cassie. When I looked at her, I always had to blink and double take just to check she really was alive and opposite me, and that this wasn't some kind of mad trick.

"What?" she asked.

I shook my head. I couldn't stop myself smiling even though all I could taste were my tears. "I just... I just can't believe it."

"Pull yourself together, little bro. It's weird for me too."

The way she joked and smiled like that reminded me of how it used to be between us when we were younger. The games we'd play. The dens we'd create together when we were camping upstate. The stories she'd tell me in the middle of the night, both terrifying and fascinating.

I wasn't going to lose her again.

"We need to get out of here," I said.

Cassie nodded. "That much is clear." She spoke like she

understood everything that'd happened, like she was conscious of what'd gone on. "What about him?"

She tilted her head across the floor.

When I saw where she meant, I felt the hairs on my arms stand on end.

Saint lay flat on the floor. He was completely still. Smoke rose from his body. I wasn't sure he was dead, but he was definitely in a bad shape, and that was enough for now. "We won't have to worry about him. Not when we've got out of this place."

"You got a plan?" Cassie asked.

I nodded. "Something like that."

The pair of us walked out through the door of the room and into the dark corridor. We rushed through it, then headed into the room where many of the humans were stacked up just waiting to be awoken, for their brainwashed, zombie-fied lives to begin.

They were still lying there. I knew I'd have to do something to get them out of here before I destroyed this place and made it disappear. I just had to hope I had the strength in me to do that.

But of course I did. I was Kyle Peters. I was Glacies.

And my ULTRA sister was beside me.

I grabbed her hand and we ran out of this room toward the corridor, which would lead us up and out of Saint's tower.

"You know where the exit is?"

"With our powers, we don't need an—"

I heard a blast. It crashed past me, past Cassie.

When I looked out of the door into the main area of Saint's tower, I saw exactly what'd caused that blast.

All of Saint's ULTRAbots were gathered around the middle of the tower. Alarms rang out through the tower. Red lights flashed. I knew this was some kind of emergency signal, triggering a meltdown.

"Hope you planned for this," Cassie said.

I held my breath. "Would it upset you if I told you I'm just winging it?"

Cassie smiled. "Not really. You were always a good winger."

I smiled back at her.

Then I turned to the mass of ULTRAbots, all of their weapons charging and ready to fire.

"When they shoot, push back."

"What?"

"Just push back. Push back with all the anger and love you have."

"How do you know it'll—"

Cassie didn't finish speaking.

The ULTRAbots fired their weapons.

I gritted my teeth and raised my hands. I tried to see the things that made me angry, but in their place, I saw love.

I saw my sister.

I saw the people I cared about.

I kept on pushing back against the oncoming mass of ULTRAbot bullets.

I tried to slow them down and stop them but they didn't seem to be losing their pace. For a moment, I was convinced I'd made a grave error. That Cassie was going to be taken away from me again just moments after we'd been reunited.

But no. I couldn't let that happen.

I threw all my powers back at those bullets.

They froze in midair. Hovered in front of my face, in front of Cassie's face. I realized then that she was pushing back, too. Both of us were holding them off, doing what we had to do to protect each other.

"Now what?" Cassie winced.

I turned my focus to the ULTRAbots. "Now we fight back."

I pushed the ULTRAbot bullets right back toward the ULTRAbots.

I saw some of the ULTRAbots try to dodge them. I saw them try to worm away.

But they didn't make it.

None of them made it.

The bullets slammed through the surrounding ULTRAbots.

All of them blasted apart, one by one, like fireworks cracking in the night sky.

From left to right, I watched as yellow flashes of light filled Saint's tower. I watched these metallic beasts erupt, then fall to the floor below.

I watched Saint's army fall apart at the hands of my sister and me, and I'd never felt happier than right now.

When they'd all fallen, there was a strange silence to the place, except for the alarm still ringing out. I took Cassie's hand. "Come on. We need to get out of here while we still can—"

"Wait!"

I heard the voice to my right. I wasn't sure who it'd come from. I thought I recognized it from somewhere, but I couldn't be certain.

When I looked closer though, I saw exactly who it was.

Nycto—Daniel Septer—my biological brother, was locked up in a cell. His hands were on the bars. He looked totally worn down. Totally dejected. "Don't leave me in here. Please."

I felt fire burn in my chest. Daniel had betrayed me. Not only that, but his betrayal had caused Orion to die. "You watched him die. You let it happen. You aren't going anywhere—"

"I made a mistake!"

I walked off, my sister beside me. "Too right you did."

"Kyle, I thought I could rule. I thought the world could be mine."

"That's where you were wrong."

"But when we spent time together. When I... when I spent

time with the Resistance and fought by your side, that was real. None of it was fake. I... I started to see your side of things. I started to want what you were fighting for. And I messed up. I messed the hell up and I'm sorry."

I gritted my teeth and resisted the urge to walk back to Daniel's cell and freeze him for eternity. "You should've thought about that before you let our dad disappear into a void."

"I have. I've thought about it a hell of a lot. And I swear I'll do everything I can to reverse what happened to Orion. I swear I'll do what I can. I just... I need a chance. A chance to make it up to you. A chance to make it up to myself. I need you to—to forgive me. Please."

I turned around. I walked back over to Daniel's cell. "You want me to forgive you?"

"Kyle, we have to go," Cassie said.

I ignored her and stood right in front of Daniel's cell. Daniel was opposite me, hands on the bars. "After everything that happened, you want me to forgive you?"

"Saint was double-crossing me. Soon after he added you to the brainwashing program, he was going to throw me into the mix so we had a hold of humanity forever. You weren't supposed to break out of that. None of us were. So you must be stronger than he thought."

"I am stronger than he thought. But that doesn't let you off the hook. Not in the slightest. Goodbye, Daniel."

I turned around and walked away.

"Forgive me. Please."

I ignored him at first. But then a memory flashed in my mind. Words Orion had said when we'd been training for our fight against Saint.

"Forgiveness burns a much brighter light than the black void of vengeance."

I didn't want to believe him then and I didn't want to

believe him now. But in this battle, I'd seen the damage and the hate blind vengeance caused. I'd seen the power forgiveness could have.

"Please," Daniel said. "Don't leave me here to rot."

"We need to go," Cassie said. There was sadness and uncertainty in her eyes.

I turned around and looked back at Daniel's cell.

"Forgiveness burns a much brighter light than the black void of vengeance."

I walked over to Daniel's cell.

Every instinct in my body told me to shove my hands through those bars and freeze him for good.

I lifted my hands. Pointed them at him. Felt the lust for vengeance at a tipping point.

"Please," Daniel said.

I turned my hands to the side and dragged the cell door away.

I threw it across Saint's tower. There was nothing between me and Daniel now. Nothing at all.

"Come on," I said. "Let's get out of here."

Daniel looked shocked. His eyes were wide. "Thank you. I... I'm so grateful. I'm so—"

"Yeah yeah. Let's leave before I change my mind."

I turned around and ran back to Cassie. Together, the three siblings of Orion, we made our way toward the top of Saint's tower.

We were almost ready to leave when we heard footsteps behind us.

When I turned around, my stomach sank.

"Leaving so soon?"

Saint stood opposite us.

His mask had been torn from his burned face.

Massive spheres of energy grew in his hands.

50

"How nice. A little family reunion. Kind of sweet, I suppose. And fitting that you'll all fall together."

Saint walked toward me, Cassie, and Daniel. We held our ground, as much as I wanted to get away. The energy ripping across Saint's hands as his tower collapsed all around us wasn't something to be messed with. I knew what he was capable of. I knew the risk he posed whenever he was near.

I knew just how strong he was.

His footsteps echoed against the metal walkways as he got closer. I could smell burning. I knew I needed to act fast if I wanted to save the brainwashed humans he had imprisoned in here.

"So how does it feel, hmm? The old gang, all reunited."

"It's over, Saint," I said.

Saint shook his head. The energy in his hands grew bigger, more threatening. "See, I don't think it is over. I don't think it's over at all. Because you're too forgiving. I mean, even after what Daniel here allowed to happen to Orion, still you forgive him."

"I should've seen what you were a long time ago," Daniel said.

Saint tilted his head to one side. Although his face was burned badly, I could tell he was smiling. "And you really trust him, do you? You really trust Daniel not to make a power grab the second I fall? You don't see this for what it really is?"

I had to admit I'd considered that this might all be some kind of ploy. Surely it was only right to be a little skeptical.

But a part of me just kept on hearing Orion's words echo around my mind.

"Forgiveness burns a much brighter light than the black void of vengeance."

I just had to hope my forgiveness was well placed.

"You might think you're strong, the three of you. You might think you can take the world for yourself. But you'll encounter problems. Difficulties will arise. And you'll see why I've had to make many decisions I've made. You'll know why I've done what I've had to do."

"You haven't had to do a thing," I spat. "You've chosen this world. You chose to brainwash humans. To hunt down ULTRAs. You chose it because you're weak."

Saint's smile twitched. "I'm weak, am I?"

"Yes. You're weak because you don't trust people or ULTRAs to follow you. So you have to resort to dirty tricks to get them onside. You're the ultimate coward."

"That's what you think the paradise I want is? A dirty trick?"

"I think it's worse. I think calling it a dirty trick is very kind. I think your 'paradise' is psychotic."

Saint took another step nearer. His footsteps sounded even heavier. I knew it was because of the energy spheres in his hands.

"No matter how idealistic a view you have of how this is all going to work out for you, you're wrong. You're wrong about everything. And you're sounding like a weak man with no options left but to make empty threats."

Saint paused for a second. He didn't say a word.

Then, "Empty threats?"

He brought the two spheres of energy together. Their light was so bright I could barely look into them. A crackling sound split through the tower as more of them fell around us. We didn't have long to get out of this place. We had to move fast.

"How's this for an empty threat?" Saint said.

The energy in front was so big that it was sucking me toward it.

"Here we are, just as Orion and I stood all those years ago. Now you can attempt to kill me by using your powers to fly at me, finishing what Orion started. But please know that if you step within inches of me, you'll be incinerated, and so too will every single human in this tower. So go on. Do what you have to do. Because only by flying through this sphere of energy with everything you have, will you kill me. But you'll die and you'll sacrifice everyone else in the process, of course. Are you willing to make that kind of sacrifice, Kyle? 'Glacies'? Does your family really mean as much as you say it does? Or are you really just all words?"

I looked at Cassie. I saw her shaking her head, tears in her eyes.

Then I looked past her at Daniel.

There was something different about Daniel. He was staring right at Saint, at that growing energy ball. The walls around us crumbled and moved toward that energy. It was growing stronger by the second.

"Have you got it in you, Kyle Peters?" Saint shouted.

"Daniel," I said.

He looked at me. His face was pale. "I have to."

"Daniel, no!"

Daniel charged up his powers.

Then he threw himself at that ball of energy.

I watched him get nearer to it. I held Cassie as I prepared for the explosion to ripple through Saint's tower; the explosion that ended Saint for good, taking us down in the process.

I saw Daniel sacrificing himself for me, and I saw the value of forgiveness all over again.

I knew what I had to do.

I took a deep breath. "I love you, sis."

"Kyle, what—"

I flew toward Saint. I was at Daniel's side in a flash. He glanced at me, then I glanced back at him and nodded.

I flew closer to Saint and readied myself to fly into him. If it protected my family, then I had to do it. It was a sacrifice I had to make.

But I noticed something by my side. When I looked around, I saw Cassie was by my side too. All three of us were now powering at that mass of energy, stronger than anything we'd ever witnessed.

All of our powers were charged up to the max.

"Go," I shouted. "I've got this."

Then Cassie took my hand.

And Daniel took my other hand.

"We're family," Cassie said.

"We're in it to the end," Daniel said.

I felt a tear roll down my cheek and I looked ahead of that enormous sphere of energy.

All of us tightened our hands.

"I love you," I shouted.

"Love you too, brother," Daniel shouted back.

"I love you too," Cassie said.

I felt the collective love of the three of us intensify our powers.

I put all my focus, all my strength, all my energy onto Saint's mass of energy.

Then it wrapped around me, swallowed me up, and there was nothing but bright, warm light as I held on to Cassie and Daniel's hands.

THE LIGHT DIDN'T last for long.

Soon, there was darkness.

But I was still awake.

I HOVERED ABOVE SAINT.

By my side, Daniel and Cassie.

Saint's spheres of power had gone.

In their place, an enormous wormhole into nothingness.

"Still not believe in the power of forgiveness?" I asked.

Saint looked scared. For a split second, he actually looked scared.

That's when I knew I'd done what I had to do.

I kicked him down into the wormhole.

I watched him fall into it, screaming as the electrical storms ripped the last of his armor away.

I watched him shrink as he tried to use his powers to cling back on the outside.

But together, me, Daniel, and Cassie focused on closing that wormhole.

Closing it for good.

"You'll regret this!" Saint screamed. "All of you, you'll regret..."

The wormhole snapped shut.

Saint's voice went silent.

When the wormhole closed, I fell to my knees.

And in the middle of the ocean surrounding Saint's falling tower, the waves now still, the sun glowing against the water, I closed my eyes, and finally, I felt at peace.

51

T*wo days later...*

IT DIDN'T TAKE the world long to rediscover its spirit.

The sun shone brightly down on Staten Island. It was quieter than I remembered. Usually, when you were anywhere around the greater New York area, you could always hear that tangible buzz in the city, and feel it in your bones. Not now. There was a solitude about the place. Not of the bad kind, though. Sure, Saint had left the world a shell of what it used to be. But it was a silence of people getting back to grips with their lives, settling back into their homes, taking things one step at a time.

Saint wouldn't be bothering anyone anymore. I'd made sure of that.

So too had my brother and sister.

"I'm not sure I can do this."

I looked to my left. Cassie stood by my side. It was still

weird, standing beside her. It didn't feel real, or like it should be happening at all. We'd been apart for so long that I'd just accepted she was gone. I put my hand on her back. "You can. You have to."

"It's just weird being back here," she said, shaking her head. "Back where it... where it ended."

"Hey," I said, looking around my street. "I like to think this is where it all started. And right now... right now, we're just picking up where we left off."

Cassie smiled at me. "You always were mature for your age."

"Unlike you," I said. "You must've lost, what, eight years in that sleep of yours?"

She punched my arm playfully. "Get screwed."

We giggled together. It sparked warmth inside. I wanted to just speak with my sister forever.

But there were people to see.

There were reunions ahead.

I looked over at my house and swallowed a sickly lump in my throat. I couldn't help being nervous about seeing my family again. They had no idea I was still alive. So God knew how they'd react to finding Cassie alive.

Truth be told, we all should've been dead when we'd flown toward Saint's sphere of energy. We'd flown into him willing to sacrifice all our lives.

But something had happened. Maybe it was that willingness to die that gave us the strength to live, bound by pure, total love.

We'd found a strength between us to fight the sphere of energy, to diminish it, and then to toss Saint away into an infinite wormhole for the rest of his existence, however long that was.

Like I said, he wouldn't be bothering anyone again.

"Maybe you should go first," Cassie said.

"You sure?"

She nodded. "If Dad's anything like he used to be then he'll jump through the ceiling when he sees I'm home."

I smiled. "Yeah. He's pretty much how he used to be."

I walked on toward the front of my house. Across the street, I saw people smiling, families reunited as their brainwash had been lifted. My legs were like jelly. I wasn't sure I could do this.

When I reached my house, I realized I didn't have a choice.

Dad was at the front door. The door was open. In the hallway, I saw Ellicia and her parents. Damon and his parents, and Avi and his parents too.

They were all chatting to one another, catching up on the horrors they'd been through, no doubt.

I didn't want to disturb them. I didn't want to intervene.

Then Ellicia's eyes met mine.

They locked for a few seconds. I swore someone said something, but I didn't know who. All sounds disappeared. Everything disappeared.

Ellicia pointed at me, then ran to me.

After her, Damon followed. Then Avi followed.

And after them, Dad followed.

"You're alive," Ellicia said, wrapping her arms around my neck. I felt the tears on her cheeks rub against my face as we held one another, as the mass of people I loved crowded around me. "You—you're alive."

I held on. Looked Avi in his smiling face, Damon in his tearful eyes. And then I looked at Dad, whose smile was larger than any I'd ever seen. "Of course I'm alive. Didn't think you'd got rid of me that easily, did you?"

"I kept—I kept the book for you, boss," Avi blubbered. He was holding on to the crinkled pages of what looked like a dating guide. "The one with the—the Goodreads reviews. The 4.1 stars."

I grabbed the book and patted Avi on his back. Then I moved on to Damon, looked into his eyes a few seconds.

"Come here," he said.

He grabbed me and squeezed me in a big bear hug. And as we reunited, it was only then that I remembered I had another reunion to make. Another person to introduce.

I looked into my dad's eyes. He put a hand on my shoulder. "My boy," he said. "My brave boy."

He hugged me, his chest shaky, and I hugged him back.

When he pulled away, I cleared my throat.

"Dad, there's—there's someone else here. Someone you have to meet."

I turned around and pointed over at Cassie, who stood alone in the middle of the road, right at the spot the Great Blast had taken her away from us.

Dad looked over at her. He narrowed his eyes. He didn't seem to recognize her.

Then confusion spread across his face.

He went completely pale and staggered to one side. "It can't be... it—it can't be—"

"It's Cassie," I said. "She never died, Dad. She's still here with us after all this time. She's still here."

Dad stumbled from side to side, and I wondered if telling him was such a good idea after all.

Cassie stood still, just staring at Dad.

And then Dad regathered his composure and he ran toward Cassie.

"My girl," he said. "My—my angel. My angel."

"Dad," Cassie said, as she collapsed into Dad's arms. "I'm here, Dad. I'm here."

"My angel," Dad cried, on his knees. "My sweet angel."

I watched the pair of them hold one another through tearful eyes. I heard sniveling all around me. I wanted to go over there and hold on to both of them, but I let them have their moment. It was a moment neither of them thought they'd ever have again.

I felt a hand grab mine. When I looked, I saw Ellicia by my side.

"You said you'd come back," she said. "You said you'd protect me. No matter what."

I nodded. "I wouldn't lie about a thing like that."

"You made it back just in time," Damon said, clamping a hand on each of our backs. "The new Mission Impossible movie got delayed 'cause of all that, y'know, Saint stuff. But now it's here. And I'm hearing this time, Ethan takes on his very first ULTRA. How frigging cool does it get?"

I laughed with Damon, Ellicia, and Avi. I felt the joy of a normal life with my friends returning. A life I never thought I'd have the chance to live again. I looked at Dad and Cassie still holding one another, and as the sun shone down on our Staten Island street, I wasn't sure I'd ever had it so perfect.

At the corner of the street, I saw a dark, hooded figure. I didn't have to see his face to know it was Daniel Septer.

He half-smiled at me. Nodded.

I took a deep breath and nodded back at him.

Then he turned around and walked away.

I looked up at the sky. Orion was right. Forgiveness really did burn a much brighter light than the black void of vengeance. I owed him so much for making me as strong as I was right now. I owed him for teaching me what I needed to know to take down Saint for good.

But right now, I had family to be with.

Real family.

"I'll be a minute," I said.

I let go of Ellicia's hand and I walked toward Dad and Cassie.

I walked toward the warm sunlight.

I walked toward their arms, and we held each other on the spot where the Great Blast took everything away from us all those years ago.

It didn't feel like an ending anymore.

More like a beginning of a new start.

A beginning of a new life.

52

"So he's definitely gone rogue?"

"He's as rogue as he damned well gets. Can't wait to beat his head to a pulp."

"Man, seriously. Tone down the rhetoric."

"What? It's what we're all thinking."

I stood in the dark harbor just outside New York. The skies were clear, and it was a humid summer night.

All around me, the rest of the remaining Resistance stood.

Ember.

Vortex.

Roadrunner.

And Stone.

"You've gone particularly angry since you took a nuclear explosion to the body," Vortex said. "That's all I'm saying."

Stone looked at his arms. He'd broken and fragmented in places, but he was still standing. The mad bastard was still standing, just like he always was. "Have you ever known me not be angry?"

Vortex tilted her head to one side. "Fair point."

"Anyway," Roadrunner said, standing in the middle of the group. "The fact is, we've got a rogue ULTRA on our hands. He's going around causing chaos. Blowing shit up. Being an all round douchebag. Typical rogue ULTRA things. He calls himself Ignite."

"Ignite?" Stone said. "Seriously? I'll ignite something in him. I'll ignite my damned fist in his jaw."

"Now that doesn't even make sense," Vortex said.

Stone didn't seem too fazed by Vortex's throwback.

"So we bring him in," Roadrunner said. "He shouldn't be too hard to deal with. But we don't want him causing any more damage. Right, Glacies?"

I stood opposite my army. The Resistance. We were government approved, now. Our duty was to protect humanity. To use our own discretion to decide what was threatening and what wasn't. We'd signed treaties. Agreed to terms that were perhaps a little restrictive.

But we were the new security for the world.

And we'd do everything we could to deal with any threats to peace that headed humanity's way.

I looked to my left. Cassie stood by my side. She was dressed in a black suit. Her hands sparked with purple electricity. "You agree?"

Cassie nodded. The electricity spread up her arms. "Whatever it takes."

Then I looked to my right.

Nycto stood there. He was dressed in an upgraded version of his old suit. Spheres of orange energy burned from his palms. "And you?"

Nycto smiled. "You know where I stand, bro. By your side. Always."

"Unless always was last year, when you were kicking his ass," Ember said.

I grinned. Then I looked back at Roadrunner and the rest of the Resistance and I nodded. "Then that settles it."

I grabbed my sister's hand, then I grabbed my brother's hand. All of the Resistance joined in after that, all of us connected. And then I looked up into the sky and saw the love and respect I had for these people open up a massive wormhole right to our destination.

"You ready?" I shouted.

"Of course we are, kid," Stone said. "Just get the hell on with it."

I looked at Nycto. Then I looked at Cassie. "Then let's do this."

I closed my eyes.

Teleported us all through that wormhole, through into whatever conflict lay ahead.

Whatever it was, it wouldn't phase us.

Nothing would stop us.

Because we were ULTRAs.

We were the Resistance.

We were The Last Heroes.

WANT MORE FROM MATT BLAKE?

The fourth book in The Last Hero series, Revenge of the ULTRAs, is now available.

If you want to be notified when Matt Blake's next novel in The Last Hero series is released, please sign up for the mailing list by going to: http://mattblakeauthor.com/newsletter Your email address will never be shared and you can unsubscribe at any time.

Word-of-mouth and reviews are crucial to any author's success. If you enjoyed this book, please leave a review. Even just a couple of lines sharing your thoughts on the story would be a fantastic help for other readers.

mattblakeauthor.com
mattblake@mattblakeauthor.com

Made in the USA
Coppell, TX
26 October 2021

64737883R00142